ABANDON

TRANSLATED BY

ABANDON

SANGEETA BANDYOPADHYAY

ARUNAVA SINHA

TILTED AXIS PRESS

রূ Roo

Names take on an added significance in this novel.

Roo is an affectionate form of the word *ruho*, the Bangla version of the Arabic *ruh*, meaning 'spirit' or 'soul', and a diminutive for the name Mahiruho. In Bangla, *ruho* functions as a suffix denoting the characteristic or nature of an object. *Mahi* is the earth, so Mahiruho is something of the earth – in this instance, a giant tree! – making Ruho both the shortened form of a giant tree, and his mother Ishwari's soul (Ishwari being the name of the all-powerful Goddess, the divine mother, the feminine principle of the world).

And then we proceed to wander around the city in search of shelter. We drift through the morbid yellow afternoon. Before our eyes, dusk descends like the trilling of a fire-engine bell and night falls like flames being extinguished by jets of water, a night as conspicuous as the whirling black skirts of desert gypsies. As for us, we are still spinning on our feet. We, that is to say, Roo and I. I, Ishwari, and Roo, who is my soul, stall for a moment in mid-air on our downward plummet. And when it is eleven-thirty (not midnight, for midnight is the hour of extreme longing for injured birds), a hallucinogenic silence surfaces on the city's streets from the netherworld.

Roo digs his nails into my thigh fearfully as I climb without hesitation into the taxi parked in the darkness beneath a tree and ask the driver, 'Will you take us?'

The young man, his hair like a bunch of black grapes, nods, he will take us. The taxi begins to move, and with our desperate attempts to seek shelter for the night, a novel begins. A malevolent, repressive, unpalatable novel. It begins to answer the question, *what is the meaning of life?* And by the time it ends, a virtual human being with transformed proclivities will have to admit that *life is constantly being a murderer!*

Roo has asked me several times, where shall we go now? I haven't answered. I have decided to look at him with impenetrable eyes if he asks again. That will be enough to shut him up. The next moment he asks me, gazing at me with his big eyes, and I am unable to be as curt as I had planned. Instead, I draw him closer. My famished love showers blessings on him and my feelings are reflected on my face. I can see my expression in a non-existent mirror. A mirror that reflects Ishwari back at me all the time, an Ishwari continuously slipping off her point of equilibrium. To make room for a narrative combining me, Ishwari, this novel and Roo, the mirror lets me hear Ishwari answer Roo as she winds up the car window. 'We'll get there, we'll find a place,' Ishwari is saying. 'We'll get there eventually. Don't worry, Roo, I am with you.'

'But where, Ma?' Roo asks like a germ.

Had it been me, I would have said, *nowhere except a place where my art will find fulfilment.* But Ishwari says, 'Where we are going now,' and Roo feels even more beleaguered by this riddle. He is already weakened from lack of food and sleep – an overdose of vulnerability from the difficult journey has left him even more lifeless. A grave sense of crisis has made him

slump on the seat of the taxi, his head drooping on
my arm. He looks as though he has been beaten up
unmercifully. And he was: in the early hours of morning his arm was trailing outside the train window
when the heavy wooden shutters slammed into his
wrist. His screaming woke me up. Roo's wrist swelled
up within minutes. For ten hours he has wandered
with me, his wrist a poisonous blue. He screamed just
once on impact but hasn't cried at all since. Perhaps
he has inherited my traits in this respect. I don't cry
either, I never have. When Ishwari cries, I purse my
lips. Every time I have the urge to cry, I tell myself
the present outcome alone isn't sufficient reason to
cry. I need more time, for time matures the outcome,
and it is this tolerance that creates the atmosphere of
this novel – this novel of truth and lies, this novel that
resembles a bird of prey.

The taxi speeds down the road while I look out
of the window. Ishwari has not managed to tend to
Roo's wrist though several hours have gone by. It
is bitterly cold and so late at night – the city roads
are empty, bereft of human bustle, everyone seems
to have sunk into a melancholy hibernation – it is
as though no one will wake again. It feels like the
moment before an explosion. I found this taxi a few
steps from the house of someone I know, someone I

approached for shelter as a last resort and was rejected by moments earlier – the third time today that this has happened. I turn to look at the house from the taxi, and from behind a curtain, someone seems to be watching us.

There was no hope of getting a taxi at this hour of night, especially on this road deep inside Jodhpur Park. I would have had to walk holding Roo's hand if I hadn't found this one. I know where Ishwari would have walked on blistered feet late into this freezing night with her child. She might have been raped, and robbed, and even if the midnight predators had left her alive, Roo would still have been separated from his mother. Ishwari would never have found her son again.

I close my eyes for a moment. Lifting his head, Roo asks, 'They won't tell us to go away from where we're going now, will they?'

What answer can I give? I am about to say, *Why did you come away like this with me? All I wanted was a glimpse of you. Why did you run away with me without telling anyone? There is no room for me to live with you anywhere in your first city, or my second city, or this third city. Can you tell me where I should take you now?*

But Ishwari doesn't give me the chance to speak. Kneading Roo's soft cheeks with both hands, she says,

'We won't go to anyone's house any more, Roo. We'll go somewhere where we can pay to stay, for as long as we like.'

Pleased at this, Roo rubs his chin on Ishwari's breast and tilts his head. 'Do you have money?' he asks. With a quick look at the taxi driver from the corner of her eye, Ishwari places a hand on her son's head like a hawk spreading its wing. But will it really be possible to secure a roof for the night in exchange for money at this hour on this winter's night? Will any of the guest houses in this city agree to rent a room to a woman unaccompanied by a man? The five-star hotels may not ask questions but will certainly ask for identification, and what identity could I possibly offer so that I am accepted by an ancient civilization? Besides, do I have enough money to seek shelter at such a hotel?

I am ravenous, but not once has Roo mentioned being hungry. I gave him a couple of biscuits before entering the last place we tried, but even that was an hour and a half ago. I wasn't thinking straight, or I could easily have got hold of bananas or chocolate. It is far too late now. There isn't a shop open anywhere.

I am surprised. How has Roo learnt to control hunger?

Roo is staring out of the window, his back stiff,

but I know he isn't looking at anything. His eyes have been empty since yesterday. When he first threw himself into my arms, crying out 'Ma!', his eyes brimmed with tears, but his joy disappeared soon after I put him down. I know what he is thinking now with his back so rigid. We spent the previous night on the train – tonight the night has closed in much further on us.

Did Ishwari ever imagine that the doors would be slammed one after the other on their misfortune? Everyone Ishwari turned to was well-established, safe in their respective home, all of them pillars of society living within a ring of security – although Ishwari now knew that none was any less helpless than she, nor any less ineffective. They were just as afraid, terrified, callous and self-centred as the destitute Ishwari and her child. And they had no conscience. Despite the peaks these people had scaled, their assets were devoted only to shoring up their own existence.

The first person I went to after getting off the train is a respected businessman in this city, exceedingly wealthy. The person I turned to on my second attempt is an influential lawyer. The third – the resident of Jodhpur Park – is a great poet, a lover of children who writes distressed poetry for the exploited: those evicted for poverty, robbed of their land, bombed, turned into victims of war. But like the awakening conscience of society, even this poet offered only compassionate rejection.

As we drifted from one address to the next, it occurred to me over and over again that the relationships that form between people every day are actually small, flourishing dreams – short-lived, fragile as glass. Like the three men who have turned her way, Ishwari averts her eyes from the helplessness of her limitations. Roo has not looked at me accusingly even once. He is probably the only one at my side during this terrible time. He came with me even though I did not want him to. He was eager to reclaim the mother who once abandoned him. I cannot understand how the five-year-old Roo can trust such a mother.

Roo was waiting for me on a secret road, holding a storybook. He is a baby, after all, he forgot to put on socks with his boots, and now he has blisters on the soft skin of his ankles. In the evening I saw the blisters had burst, the pink flesh visible beneath the scraped-off skin. Roo has endured it all in silence.

'Does it hurt very much, Roo?' Ishwari asked, turning his face towards her.

Roo shook his head quickly, no, it wasn't hurting at all. Ishwari's eyes smarted and I remember that it is time to tell the taxi driver where to go.

I remember a small guest house on Lansdowne

Road and request the driver to take us there. As I speak, I realise my voice is trembling, as is my heart, with all kinds of anxieties. How deserted these roads are. I feel a surge of anger as I observe the countless dark, indifferent houses on either side – don't any of them have a little space for me? Ishwari is freezing – Roo had come away without warm clothes and she has wrapped him in her own shawl. By way of a second warm garment, we have a sleeveless jacket, which I am wearing. I have discarded many of my possessions in the hope of shedding my burden. I have a light blanket – but you can hardly walk on the road wrapped in a blanket. And why not? Is it because it's different from what society considers normal?

Shaking off the dominating cold, I give instructions to the young man driving us and the taxi arrives at the guest house. The word 'lodging' is written in small letters in one corner of the neon signboard. It appears extremely significant to me. I count out forty rupees for the driver. Forty rupees is a lot of money for me now. Roo gets off the taxi after me, awkward in the shawl wrapped around him. As I accept the change, I wonder how long Roo and I can survive on the money I have. I wonder but cannot make an estimate. Then again, what's the use? I never think too much of what's possible and what isn't; on the contrary, I'm more interested in the performance a person puts on when poised between the possible and the impossible. And precisely for this reason, I feel a sense of satisfaction from comparing intellect, genius and foolishness when I come across a flawed individual. By those standards Ishwari is my least favourite person, for she is everything I am not. Ishwari is Roo's mother – the same Roo whose touch is unbearable to me.

Walking up to the gate of the guest house after retrieving her suitcase and canvas bag from the taxi, Ishwari found it padlocked. There was no one to be seen anywhere. Putting her luggage down on one side and motioning to Roo to stand next to it, Ishwari swept her eyes over the gate, trying to spot a doorbell. Rattling the gate, I say loudly, 'Anyone here? Hello? Anyone?' No one responds.

I realise the taxi hasn't left. I should have asked the driver to wait, I tell myself, because if we don't get a room here we'll have to go somewhere else quickly. We have no choice but to find a sanctuary or spend the rest of the night in the taxi looking for one.

I glance behind me and am surprised to see that the young man has got out of the taxi and is leaning against it, observing us closely. The sight relieves me and also makes me frown. Without deliberating over it too much I go up to him and say, 'I'm glad you didn't leave. It doesn't look like we'll get a room here – it would really help if you waited a little longer.'

'I'm here,' came the brief reply. It was enough. For the moment, Ishwari just needed a little assurance, a little support. Some sort of third presence besides her own and Roo's. It was freezing outside – Roo should have remained in the taxi, the shawl was unable to protect him from this bitter wind. But Ishwari was forced to reject the idea the very next moment. What if the young man started the car and sped away with Roo? And sold him to an Arab sheikh? And made him a jockey for camel races in the desert? And Roo fell on the sand as soon as the camel leapt up to gallop off? And kicked by hundreds of galloping camels, was tossed about between their hooves like a lump of flesh in a dust storm? Forgetting where she was, Ishwari remained rooted to the spot for a few moments – the young man suddenly appeared terrifying. I scold Ishwari, I force her to lower her eyes and return to the locked gate of the guest house, where her son stands. I rattle the gate with all my strength. I keep rattling it. At the core of this auto-deconstruction within the vortex of speculation lies a recent incident. An incident that is a story.

—

Ishwari ran out of drinking water on the train yesterday evening, and although they passed two or three stations, no one came by peddling bottled water. Roo began to stir, restless with thirst. Ishwari gave him two sips of water from the bottle of the man next to her, but he asked for more again few minutes later, and grew agitated when he didn't get any. When the train stopped at Bhogpur — a deserted railway station — she got off after instructing Roo repeatedly to stay where he was. Ishwari spotted water dripping from a broken-down tap in the distance. She did not have patience to fill her bottle to the top, it would have taken too long. Rushing back to her compartment with the bottle half-full, she discovered that Roo was missing. He was nowhere to be found. She combed the entire compartment but did not find Roo anywhere, nor the man who had sat next to her. She had remembered he had got on the train at Bilaspur.

Ishwari wanted to weep. She wanted to tear out her hair. She asked everyone whether they had seen Roo, no one could give her any information. Abandoning her luggage, she jumped off the train and called out his name at the top of her voice: 'Roo! Roo! Roo!'

The train whistled and lurched forward. 'Roo.' Her cries rent the air. At that moment she thought of something she had wanted to tell him, but would never be able to if he were not found, piled up caresses that would weigh down on her like a mountain if Roo were lost to her.

Suddenly she thought she heard someone call out 'Ma!' from another compartment. Recognizing it at once as his voice, she raced off in the direction of the sound and found a scared and bewildered Roo standing in front of the bath-room near the third compartment. He fell into a deep sleep as soon as he saw her. And how unnaturally he slept. When he awoke, all he could say in response to her many questions was, 'The uncle sitting next to you gave me a Coke.' Ishwari did not ask further. For she had realised that this 'uncle' would always be hovering near them. She realised that this uncle's real name was 'danger'.

—

The clang of a gate being shaken became audible. Perhaps the birds hidden in the trees had grown res-tive at the disturbance. The sound of wings being fluttered could be heard in one or two trees. And with it a single light – signalling the intent to illumi-nate Ishwari's entire surroundings – came alive in the room adjoining the passage.

When he sees the light, Roo comes up and nes-tles against me. One end of his shawl is trailing in the dust. I am startled. The shawl is quite valuable. Selling it might fetch a good price and I am in acute need of money now. Ishwari too can successfully counter all her resentments with money – all the resentments of the soul of this novel replete with truths and lies – resentment at not being able to find a sanctuary, for her bruises, for scraped skin, at being the victim of theft and many other such rancours that have flared up into grotesque rage before being consigned to simmering hatred.

In spite of the light, no one appears in the passage nor do we hear the sounds of anyone waking up. Hopelessly I turn around and call out, 'Do you know any other hotel or guest house nearby? Can you take me there?'

The young man walks up to us slowly. 'You should have tried much earlier. It'll be hard to find anything open now.'

'I had no choice.' Ishwari shook her head. 'I didn't realise.'

'We have a problem now,' said the young man, stuffing his hands in his pockets.

Ishwari takes control at such times. I don't like talking too much. Ishwari tries to wind words around life to tie it down. She speaks like written sentences, and in this case too she followed Derrida's prescription, that 'speech is writing' or 'speech is a complex definition of writing' and made her finishing statement.

'Problem?' said Ishwari and continued, 'I'm not

thinking of problems any more. Neither mine nor anyone else's – I'm not thinking of anyone's problems at all. I have become a stranger to this city. People who once knew me have forgotten me. I used to live here – I was a citizen of this city, a companion to it. The relationship has changed but I must build bonds with this city through problems and crises. In one sense it's a blessing no one has offered me a place to stay. You cannot survive under someone else's roof. Cheap guest houses in residential neighbourhoods such as this one are safer.'

'Provided you get a room...'

'If not here, then elsewhere.' Ishwari seemed to have a brainwave. 'And if I don't, will you take me to Howrah Station? You will be doing me a huge favour.' Yes, indeed, Howrah Station. It lacked nothing – water, food, lights, toilets.

The young man looked at her and Roo in surprise. 'You'll spend the night at the station? You call that a solution?'

'Why not? It's an excellent place. I've done it before, but on my own. This time the presence of the child makes it difficult,' Ishwari said and sighed. At that moment they heard a door being unbolted.

'Ma!' Roo called out.

The sound of the door being unlatched is so long

drawn-out that it seems the person inside had been unwilling to brave the cold to meet his guests, but eventually changed his mind. He opens the door with sluggish, heavy fingers frozen by the chill. Small guest houses such as this one are not particularly enthusiastic about strangers arriving so late at night; at this hour they are not guests, they merely seek a roof over their heads.

A hunched old man in a dhoti and shirt emerges and makes his way slowly towards the gate. His right foot is encased in a thick plaster cast. He is limping. The old man gives me hope. I am sure the padlocked gate will be opened in a moment. The old man inspects me, Roo, the young driver, the taxi and the surroundings carefully, his mouth slightly open, and then says, clearing his throat, 'We don't have a room – everything is booked till the fourth.'

The old man knows who we are, which is why he does not ask questions like 'Who are you?' or 'What do you want?'

I don't have to say anything, someone behind me speaks. 'Please make some arrangements,' he says. 'How do you expect her to go looking for a room with a child at this hour? Let her stay the night, she'll go to some other hotel tomorrow.'

It's hard to say what would have happened had I

been forced to start this conversation. I would not have been able to beg and plead. Ishwari cannot control herself, her nerves are about to collapse under the pressure. On the verge of being defeated by an overwhelming loneliness, she cannot imagine a complete stranger speaking up uninhibitedly on her behalf. At these moments the body becomes numb, I feel an urge to surrender this fleeting life in his hands and go to sleep. Ishwari, however, feels the desire to taste this release.

Ishwari looked at the young man carefully for a moment. He had a longish, dry face, small eyes and acne scars on his cheeks. There was a strange play of light and shade on those uneven cheeks, as though the pits on the skin hosted experiences that Ishwari's imagination could never reach. Ishwari shivered. It was the effect of the night. Darkness casts a supernatural shadow on the mind, although the relationship between this shadow and human society is a seductive one.

'The manager of this guest house has gone home on holiday,' says the old man helplessly. 'Had he been here, he could have taken a decision. I cannot do it. Please try to understand, you can see I'm a crippled old man. I've been rejected from employment a long time ago. Besides, we don't have any empty rooms.'

It is indeed difficult for the old man to keep standing. 'I can barely stand, but I had to come when I heard a young woman's voice.'

He is about to go back when I speak up, 'Let me sit here in this passage tonight, I'll pay for a room—'

Before I can finish, Roo astonishes us by taking a couple of steps forward and grasping the iron gate. Looking up at the old man and nodding his head, he says, 'We'll sit and we'll eat something too. We're very hungry.' He continues to nod with studied assurance, and Ishwari presses Roo's head to her thigh to make him stop.

The old man leans towards Roo. 'Hasn't the child eaten anything?' he asks.

'The train was late, you see,' I respond quickly, 'and before anything else I wanted to find a place for the night.'

'There's no arrangement for meals. You have to eat at a restaurant or order in. You don't get anything except tea and coffee here. Don't you have anything to eat?'

The question flew at her from the back like a gust of hot wind cutting through the cold. Ishwari shook her head without a backward glance. Roo has become impatient now, rubbing his eyes as he tugs at my hand. 'Come along, Ma,' he says. I am certain

Roo means we should go to Howrah Station. He has noticed that you get food there, and a place to sit. Even with his limited intelligence he has realised that Ishwari will not be able to offer better arrangements than the one at Howrah Station.

Ishwari was at her wits' end. Roo. She had no one but Roo. Countless days and nights without Roo in them haunted her like an unforgiving famine. Ishwari had spent a long time without seeing Roo, without feeling his touch. She was turning into a sprawling banyan tree with each passing day – accursed down to the roots along with the trunk and vines and leaves and boughs. She could see herself in the mirror, her eyes round like saucers, her hair red, standing on end. Ishwari had become insane with need for her son. She would nurture an emptiness as heavy as a rock, as thorny as cactus, in her arms. Sometimes she would fling her food, her crockery and her bedclothes to the ground and beat her breast in a tearless lament. And she would sing.

Patthar ka palna, kaanto ki dori
Kaise toh toru, nindia ko tori?

Your cradle is of rock, it swings on a crown of thorns
How, then, can I disturb your sleep?

I have seen all this. I know Ishwari would rather wander through the streets holding Roo by the hand than endure this agony – starving for two successive nights is nothing compared to this. Even though Ishwari now stands in the middle of the pavement, troubled and confused, looking around helplessly, happiness continues to blossom in her heart. Even though one day this novel will stop this joy in its tracks, and throttle it.

One last time Ishwari asked the old man, 'Is there really nothing you can do?'

'No, there really is no room available.' The old man shook his head again. 'A guest cannot be made to spend the night in the passage. I am helpless.'

I see the young taxi driver turn around without protest and walk back to the taxi. I am forced to return to the taxi too, holding Roo's hand. This taxi is now my real refuge. Roo is walking with his eyes shut. I say to the young man, 'I know of a hotel near Hazra Road, please take me there.' Without answering, he looks over his shoulder at me before opening the door to climb into his seat. Putting the suitcase and bag into the taxi, I get in and sit down with Roo in my lap.

At this moment I feel an urge to look out at the sky. I have never desired dawn before. I am a lover of the night, a woman who roves in the dark. My mind expands each time I put the night like a pillow over my head. I have no such expectations of dawn. Dawn signifies transparency, trustworthiness – dawn means the end of all mystery, or all romance. But tonight my inclinations have changed. Mine, or Ishwari's? At the break of dawn Ishwari will be able to roam the city freely with Roo holding her hand, she will be able to look for a room, gather some of the things she needs to survive.

The young man switched off the taxi engine after switching it on. 'There's a boarding house of sorts in my neighbourhood,' he said, 'they might be able to put you up for a few hours.'

'Oh no!' Ishwari exclaimed. 'Please take me to the hotel I told you about! If they don't have a room please take me to Howrah Station. I know I'm bothering you endlessly, but who else can I turn to at this moment? I have to save this child at any cost, and I have to save myself to save him, I cannot take too many risks. If something were to happen to me, I cannot even begin to imagine what he'll do or where he'll end up. If you're ready to take me where I want to go, I'll come with you – if not, I'm prepared to stay here on this pavement,' she declared, using the sleeve of her kurta to wipe the tears flowing down her face.

I observe the old man hobbling back.

'You can trust me,' said the young man, starting his engine.

Ishwari's head was about to drop in embarrassment, but such is the nature of this novel – it is sceptical and trusting at the same time, it tells the truth and also lies. It must be our nature too – when we leave our house keys with a stranger, we ask ourselves: what can he steal anyway?

'Then let's go to Howrah Station,' said Ishwari, smiling faintly at this person whom she had no choice but to trust. That's when I see the old man pause and turn. He raises his arm. First one, then both together. 'Just a minute,' he shouts.

Ishwari practically leapt in the air. 'He's calling us, he's calling us…' she jumped out of the taxi.

—

Ishwari hadn't requested him to do it, but the young man carried their bag and suitcase upstairs. When they climbed up the spiral staircase, he asked to take the sleeping Roo from Ishwari's arms. He took a broom from the old man and swept the room. Then, without a word to her, without even taking the fare for the taxi, he slipped away unnoticed, probably while she was busy talking to the old man. Ishwari had even forgotten to ask him his name. She felt guilty about not saying goodbye.

The old man was Gourohori Basak. He used to be the manager of the guest house, but owing to his age he didn't – or couldn't – look after the place any more. He spent all his time alone in his room. He had no roots anywhere and the owners of the guest house had not yet asked him to go back to his village. He would probably leave as soon as he was told to. The twenty-something Nikhil Biswas, who was now the manager, was a distant relative of the owner's wife's. Based on the strength of this connection he made the venerable Gourohori Basak quake in his shoes. He had displayed great strength of character in allowing Ishwari to stay on such a makeshift arrangement in Nikhil Biswas's absence. His resolve had strengthened simply out of consideration for Roo.

After tucking Roo into bed, I go downstairs with Gourohori Babu to get a packet of biscuits. He has a very hard time climbing up and down the stairs. He usually cooks himself a simple meal in a corner of his room. Since he slipped and injured his foot the day before yesterday, he has had virtually nothing to eat. The maid, who goes by the name Nepal'er Ma, and whose job it is to sweep and swab the guest house, brought him some snacks in the afternoon, which is all he has had to eat. The two boys, Prabir and Montu, who run errands in this guest house, know that Gourohori has been rejected and that Nikhil Biswas is the master of their fate. As a result, Gourohori never gets any help from them, no matter how desperate his need.

In his room, Gourohori Babu lifts the lid of an ancient aluminium trunk and brings out a packet of biscuits. 'Eat a couple yourself,' he says, using the formal *aapni* instead of the familiar *tumi*, 'and put the rest by your son's pillow. If he wakes up and asks for food, soak them in water and give them to him. It will be morning soon, I'll take an extra packet of milk and heat it up for you. You can give it to him when he wakes up. Milk is good for strength. Let's see what we can do after that.'

'Please don't address me formally,' Ishwari told Gourohori, 'you're so much older than I am.' This was the Ishwari within me, the one who was comfortable with social etiquette. My attitude is a lot like an air-hostess's; I have grasped the importance of floating high above ground level. I am organised, Ishwari is harum-scarum; I am sincere, Ishwari draws on her inner resources. I don't think there's any particular purpose to my existence, but for the last two days life has not seemed quite as meaningless to Ishwari. She has got her son back, but my misgivings about Roo have not yet been dispelled.

Gourohori refused to address Ishwari any other way. Taking off his woollen cap, he said, 'A single night's predicament does not degrade a human being. If even a single room had been available, I would have had to serve you with the same trepidation with which I serve other guests. Even at this moment, you are a guest at this guest house, while I am nothing but an employee allowed to occupy a small corner by the generosity of the owner. It does not befit me to address you in any manner other than formally.'

There was a water-filter installed in the terrace next to the passage – after filling two bottles of water, I go upstairs. The room that shelters us from the cold on this winter's night is situated above another on the top floor, with a spiral staircase leading up to it. The stairs end in a narrow corridor with a wooden railing, leading into the room whose roof is tiled. The building itself is well-maintained. The exteriors have been painted white recently, with bottle-green borders; the tiles are painted the same shade of green, the wooden railing too.

It is actually a store-room of sorts for torn mattresses and pillows. The garbage inside is nothing but tattered and shredded, rotting lumps of cotton wool.

The cot has found place here only because one of its legs is broken. Somehow Gourohori has managed to push it against the wall, place a dilapidated mattress on it, and cover it with a milk-white sheet for us to spend the night on.

As a baby, whenever Roo slept this way on his back, he would twitch repeatedly in his sleep, and Ishwari would place something heavy on her son's chest or adjust his position so he slept on his side. She was watching her son sleep after a long time.

Does motherhood find its greatest satisfaction in seeing one's child sleep peacefully? Ishwari had waited forever for such a sight. She would draw the sleeping Roo to her breast, causing him to curl into a ball, rub her cheek against his, and draw ships and ferris wheels on his eyelids...

Longing, longing, leaf by leaf
I tear my grief... When will you
Come home and play?

And her mutilated penance was just for this.

Roo looked exhausted. His mouth was slightly open. There was a touch of resentment about his lips and chin. Somewhere within him a process of hurt was under way, throbbing with unhappiness. One day

Ishwari will wipe off this pain, this resentment from her son's heart, with an effort beyond her means. My abandoning him, the growing distance month by month, my hesitation at accepting him afresh, two days of homelessness, the grief of wandering through the city, the sense of insecurity – Ishwari will absorb all these. I don't know if she will succeed; I don't know if she will survive.

How will she survive?
Her fingers are stolen, shoulders don't swim,
Another bad moon is yet to dive –
How, how will she survive?

The world is heartless. Ishwari is weak, bankrupt – unfit for battle.

I abandoned domestic life, left my child to arrive at a distant land to write a novel; toiling by day and night, I completed it. One day, as I was reading my own manuscript, there was a power-cut. I lit a candle. My eyes grew heavy as I read by candlelight. I decided to close my eyes for a minute before resuming. But as soon as I did I sank into slumber. Body and mind shutting down, I went to sleep. I didn't open my eyes till I was scalded by the impossible heat of fire.

I found my novel in flames. The fire had eaten

up half the manuscript already. The rest burned to ashes with my imagination as its witness – it was burnt completely and I did nothing but watch.

I did nothing because I was in the grips of the strongest rage. I had written the novel – surely Ishwari could have battled with the flames to save it. But Ishwari does not know how to fight; Ishwari surrenders in advance.

Still, this woman has taken Roo away in her arms. It is a very big risk. And I don't know what Ishwari will do with him now.

I need to sleep too. No one knows whether tomorrow will prove to be an even more difficult day. Tearing the packet of biscuits open, I eat two. A dim light glows in the room. What next, I wonder, hunger gnawing at my insides. I stare at the light for a clue but my mind refuses to function. Turning over on my side, I find Roo moving his jaws in his sleep. Is he eating in his dreams? Negating my indifference, Ishwari crawled up to her son, hugging him to her and squeezing him. Then, drawing him to her exhausted body, she fell asleep.

—

It was quite late when Ishwari awoke. The sunlight hadn't filtered in, however, since all five windows on the three walls were shut tight. Ishwari scolded her-self. She had intended to wake Roo early and give him something to eat. This was her principal task. Gourohori Babu had promised to arrange for some milk too.

Springing out of bed, Ishwari saw the empty packet on the floor, crinkled and shredded. She was surprised – she had eaten only two. She concluded that it must be the handiwork of a giant rat, trembling at the thought. Ishwari turned agitated and fearful eyes towards Roo's tender fingers and saw at once the profusion of brown biscuit crumbs around her son's gloomy lips.

Her heart was torn asunder. She smothered Roo in kisses. Holding him, she tried to cross the end-less desert in her soul, babbling, 'It'll never happen again, Roo, I'll never leave you and go off – we won't be separated any more. You'll forget, you'll forget those days. You'll forget how children turn home-less without their mothers, how they wander from one room to another with ashen eyes, sobbing like cats, how they glue their noses to every window and their eyes to the road, how they cannot ask for food when they're hungry, how they grope in their sleep for a body packed with compassion, the body within whose sac of cool water they had wanted to stay forever.'

'I shall wash away your hurt, your emptiness, I will strangle the betrayal you faced. You shall live, you shall live with me. We will make our union successful in every sense of the word, Roo – my Mahiruho!'

As she said this, a pair of eyes rose before her eyes. Roo rose before Roo, memories of Roo – or was it imagination or Roolessness – like a dream. In the dream, the eyes changed to grief and repentance which mingled into fat teardrops that trickled down from her eyes. Witnessing Ishwari's tears of fatigue, I realise I have always considered motherhood simply a matter of regular practice – how wrong I have been.

The moment a woman gives birth and turns into a mother, her sense of motherhood becomes infinite. Even in the case of mothers whose arms are emptied soon after delivery, their absent children continue to hover like ghosts all their lives. That is why, despite all my efforts, Ishwari's love and desire has not diminished. Roo's love has preserved the natural abundance of tears within Ishwari like a well-protected mound of grain.

Roo is sleeping – let him sleep a little longer. The room fills with sunlight when I open the windows. Glittering sunbeams hurl themselves on the dusty floor. Two sparrows chirp at one of the windows, against the steady hum of a car bustling down Lansdowne Road. I am surrounded by buildings, as though a thousand chemical solutions of life are waiting in beakers, ready to be experimented with. Each has a distinct taste, texture and smell. I begin to feel restless at the sight of these closely packed buildings – I wrote a novel of truths and lies. It was burnt to ashes, and yet another novel of truths and lies is being woven around my life. Will this one burn down too? It's bound to – for Roo is now flashing like lightning between Ishwari and me.

The truth is: I did not want to give birth to Roo. Roo's arrival was unintended. I dislike children. You could say I cannot stand them. I made any number of secret attempts to ensure that the embryo lodged in my womb was not born. The doctor said my uterus was slack, that the embryo could be shaken loose quite easily, so I should take complete rest during my pregnancy. The people I was bearing the child for, like a faithful woman of the family, decreed that I should stay in bed round the clock. They put me under strict surveillance. And without getting out of bed, I plotted ways for my undesired embryo to escape from my slack uterus. I inserted my hair into my nostrils to induce violent sneezing so that my stomach muscles could put terrible pressure on my uterus and force the foetus out. Locking myself in the bathroom, I poked a knitting needle into my vagina so that the life within could be destroyed. I collapsed immobile in bed after a hundred sit-ups, sobbed in the empty room, shaking my head violently – 'I don't want this child – I don't want it!' But I simply could not free myself of the foetus. Thwarting all my efforts, it was born a complete human being. And emerging from within me, Ishwari took him in her loving arms.

This predatory novel, like an owl in search of blood, knows the reason for my disenchantment. Like a wise psychoanalyst it knows that my life began on a stormy, rainy night in the veranda of a delivery room. To this day I have no idea who made me and then abandoned me there. Perhaps rage at this rejection rose within me at times, during moments of humiliation, when I would hit myself, drawing blood. My insistence was not on suicide but on self-flagellation. But that was a different I. Time did not spare me, though it certainly changed me.

When I was two, a childless couple chose me from a thousand others. Sakshi and Hitabrata did not have a child even after several years of marriage. I came away in their arms from the orphanage in Ranchi to Calcutta nearly twenty-five years ago. It was Hitabrata who named me Ishwari. I grew up amidst

love, care and affluence. I did not even know I was
not their biological offspring. I became the apple of
everyone's eye – Hitabrata's brother's and sister's and
Sakshi's mother's. I was afflicted, and used, by all sorts
of relationships – with uncles and aunts, parents and
grandparents. Each of these relationships imprisoned
me with its own needs. This tussle for possession over
me continued for exactly fourteen years. Then Sakshi
gave birth to her own child. And they threw me away.

After fourteen years they disowned me like garbage. I felt the wild hoofbeats of humiliation on my
sixteen-year-old body and mind. I did not grasp the
implications of this change. On her return from the
nursing home with her baby in her arms, Sakshi's first
act was to evict me from the large, well-appointed
room next to hers in which I had lived until then. I
was made to move to the ground floor. Their faces
radiated unshakeable hatred. Sakshi's mother wrinkled her face when I went near her. After kissing my
face lovingly all these years, she had only now realised
that I had sin coursing through my veins. She realised
my beauty could never have come from Hindu line-
age.

I was not allowed to touch anything in the house.
And the strictest surveillance was employed to keep
me at a distance from the newborn baby. This was the

child – Chitran – who I had come to adore at first sight.

Sixteen-year-old Ishwari experienced an extreme reaction to her love being scorned, to being assaulted mercilessly. Whenever she wanted to express her love for Chitran, the tiny compartments of her heart filled with vengefulness. She did not realise that suppressing love is the strongest form of self-flagellation in the world.

There was no shortcoming to the family's hatred. They wouldn't tolerate me another moment. There was a single demand: 'Go away, go away, go away!'

But where could Ishwari go? She had so many requirements – shelter, college fees, bus fare, books. For fourteen years I'd been trapped in a sticky and deceitful web of love and affection. I was not prepared for the indifference of existence. I was not equipped to face the brutality of the world. In my stupor, I was assaulted again and again. My life began to mock me. I consumed leftovers like a flea-ridden dog. I constantly felt impure, sullied by love, and my sixteen-year-old mind persuaded me that the only reason for my misery was that child, Chitran.

When the child was about a year old, I was driven mad with loathing for him. When he fell ill I couldn't sleep for joy. I prayed for his death. I used to dream that Chitran was dead and a crazed Sakshi would beg me for forgiveness. It was like the moral of a cautionary tale. But my heart was raw vengeance now, stripped of love and affection. My dreams knocked a howling Sakshi to the floor, stamped on her with their heels.

I grew into a quiet girl, burying my nose in the theory of velocity, immersing myself in the most difficult calculus theorems to persecute myself. I would solve geometry riders all day. Riders, riders and more riders so that my heart could grow as heavy as lead.

And in the lab I searched for poison – I was determined to create a toxin from a compound of nitrogen and a carbonate with nitrogen sulphide. Evading everyone's watchful eyes, I'd go up to Chitran, who would look at me with wide eyes and say, 'Eh?' Then he would suck on my finger. I would run away.

Gradually every child became Chitran for me: a tyrannical, obscene lump of flesh, dogged by misfortune. Long after emerging from Sakshi and Hitabrata's shadow, when I no longer even recollected their faces, nor Chitran's, I remained callous and devoid of feelings for children. Still, the image of Iswari's sobbing face in the mirror appears vividly in my mind. Ishwari sobs before the mirror because there is no one else to witness her tears.

—

Taking her towel, soap and clothes out of her bag, Ishwari climbed down the spiral staircase to the terrace. Gourohori Basak had unlocked the bathroom on the roof for her, surprised not only that he still had the key, but also that he had remembered where he'd kept it. As she brushed her teeth, Ishwari observed that besides cobwebs, the rubbish in the bathroom comprised a heap of liquor bottles. She used a stick she found on the roof to dust the cobwebs off. She didn't have to, but Roo might have been frightened by the thick, silvery threads. This reminded her that she had not locked the door to the room when leaving it. What if Roo woke up and, not seeing her anywhere, tried to climb down the winding iron staircase?

Ishwari rushed out of the bathroom. And saw her son standing halfway down the spiral staircase – just one step below him, Gourohori himself, a glass of milk in one hand, the other clutching Roo's shoulder. Gourohori's shawl had slipped off his body.

A chill ran down Ishwari's spine. 'Roo!' she exclaimed, her voice trembling.

'Quick, I can't keep my balance,' said Gourohori cautiously.

She ran up to gather Roo in her arms, toothpaste

still foaming in her mouth. She was still shaking when she entered the room, panting. Despite his injured foot, Gourohori manoeuvred his way up to the room too. 'There could have been a terrible accident,' he said. 'Why did you go out without locking the door?'

She remained sitting, stricken, her son in her lap. 'If he had slipped he'd probably have fallen all the way.'

'Never mind, nothing like that happened,' Gourohori cut in. 'If you hadn't been there…' The old man seemed angry with himself. 'You know, I could see him coming down the stairs groggily, and I couldn't even run with this injured foot.'

'You've done a great deal for us since last night, Gourohori Babu,' she said. 'I owe you a great deal.'

Gourohori put his hand on Roo's head. 'Brush your teeth or milk first, sir?' he said.

With a quick glance at his face, Roo accepted the glass of milk with both hands and gulped it down.

'Why are you crying?' asked Gourohori Babu, looking at Ishwari. 'The night is over, there's nothing to be afraid of now. And there's always a risk of accident where a child is concerned. We overcome these things to grow up, to grow old. Supposedly, I fell off my bed so many times when I was a child that my head changed shape altogether.'

'There's always a risk, Gourohori Babu,' said Ishwari, 'I probably won't be able to protect Roo. I'm not worthy – I'm not a worthy mother or a good mother. Again and again I've failed to protect him. Once, I chose to abandon him and run away instead of keeping him by my side – he had a high fever. He could barely eat. Still I sacrificed him in order to live.'

'Please be calm,' the old man tells me. 'God tests mothers in different ways. I think his injured hand should get some treatment first.' On his way out, Gourohori stopped and turned. 'You should help him have a wash. And one more thing: he's the one who will decide how good a mother you are, at the right time.' Gourohori nodded cryptically.

'Toilet, Ma,' Roo called out to her.

'Yes, let's go,' she said, and descended to the terrace, Roo in her arms. She waited outside while he used the toilet, then rubbed toothpaste on his teeth with her fingers. At this moment she had none of the things that Roo needed, not even a change of clothes. After rinsing his mouth, she gave her son a bath. He hadn't had one in three days.

And they needed food, something nourishing that would sustain them for the day. Ishwari needed some tea too. Her head felt like a ton of bricks. Her shoulders ached.

How strange life is, she mused, how long it has been since they slept on the same bed, mother and child.

Ishwari poured water over her son swiftly, rubbing soap over his arms and legs. She still had to take her own bath, after which she would have to get a doctor to examine Roo's hand. But the moment she put soap on his feet, he sobbed, 'It hurts, Ma!' The soap and water were smarting where his skin had been scraped off.

Ishwari tried to withstand Roo's pain for him, feeling once again that she could not protect him. And that her own life would prove more difficult to negotiate with Roo in it.

'I won't wear those shoes any more, Ma!' Tears streamed down Roo's cheeks.

'No, you won't, not at all. We'll buy new shoes. We'll buy slippers, all right?' She burst into tears too, her eyes locked into her son's.

Roo stared at her, his cheeks puffed up, as though he were looking deep inside her. The terrace was filled with sunshine, there was a pleasant breeze and Roo was encircled in her arms – she no longer felt godless like she had a few days ago.

Roo smiled shyly as he looked at her, placing his left hand lightly on her right breast, and lightning flashed through her soul. The fragments of her heart came together, and she kissed her son all over his face. Roo seemed unbelievably starved too, returning passion with passion. Eventually they were both exhausted. Sighing deeply with his cheek pressed against her breast, Roo said, 'I've been so sad, Ma.'

Ishwari understood his sorrow at once. She nodded violently.

Depositing Roo in the room, she locked the door and took her own bath. As she bathed, several questions about the pile of liquor bottles occurred to her. She thought of asking Gourohori Babu why these bottles were in the bathroom when he had the key to the room. And how long they had been here. Emerging from the bathroom, Ishwari was surprised by Gourohori Babu, who was waiting outside with a cup of tea.

'Here you are,' he said.

'Why must you keep climbing up and down the stairs?' she asked. 'I'd have come myself.'

'None of the boys who deliver tea to the rooms would have kept my request. So I had to come. What's a morning without a cup of tea?'

Putting down her towel, soap and toothpaste on the iron steps, Ishwari accepted the cup and took a long sip. She felt fresh now. Spreading out her wet hair, she stood with her back to the sun. She felt as though life held no problems for her any more, as though she had been living here on this terrace for a long time. Gourohori Babu showed her a clothesline to hang her wet towel out to dry. She obeyed him dutifully.

The old man sat down on the steps. 'At this age the winter sun feels wonderful,' he said with an embarrassed smile. 'But I'm stuck downstairs because I can't manage the stairs. How beautiful the city looks from here. You can pass the time just looking at it.'

'I'm going to take Roo to a doctor,' said Ishwari. 'Would you like to come too? I'll feel happy if I can do something for you.'

The old man glanced at her distantly. 'This room was occupied some time ago by a man and a woman for seven years, pretending to be a married couple! I was in charge then. The owners were abroad for years, leaving this guest house and the one on Dover Road in my care. One day I discovered that they were not husband and wife, they had eloped. She had a husband and children, he had a wife and children too. I was furious at first. Later, when my temper cooled, I realised that two people who had spent seven years together were no less than a married couple. They obviously had a bond – and the bond was all that mattered. And considering what goes on now under the supervision of the new manager, they were quite a nice couple, those two. He used to bring back snacks for her every evening. This bougainvillea here was planted by her. She used to invite me to have dinner every now and then.

'Dinratri is no longer a guest house – it's a place in a prime location in the city for spending time with alcohol and women. A cheap hotel. Five hundred rupees for two hours.

'I've stayed on simply because I have nowhere to go. By allowing you to spend a night here, I've tried to protect not your honour but the honour of the people I've lived off for forty years. No one comes to a guest house out of choice, only by necessity. If those who really need a room can't get one, what's it all in aid of?'

'But how can anyone live in a guest house for seven years?' asked Ishwari.

'In those days people used to take rooms on hire that way. Sometimes for an entire month, sometimes for three. There wasn't such a thick flow of guests twenty years ago. The rules were relaxed too. Say they're staying for ten consecutive days, you'd give them a discount of fifty rupees a day. People were eager to be generous back then. There's no doubt that times have changed enormously. This couple started out for three months but eventually stayed on for seven years. They used to cook and eat in the attic and live in the room on the terrace. The young woman filled this place with plants. The conch shell could be heard at dusk, when there were ceremonial prayers. A chap named Manmatha used to run errands for them, he'd get hold of a cow every Friday to be fed ritually. And all of us would be bribed with the chillies and tomatoes grown here on the roof.'

'We didn't discuss the charge for the room,' Ishwari said.

'Look, this Nikhil isn't a straight-talker, he has been conspiring to evict me in any case. He has even tried to put the fear of ghosts in me. If he sees you today he will create a scene. I don't have the authority to unlock this room. What shall I say about the charge? I cannot charge you. Can you charge someone for helping them in a crisis? This room is not fit to live in. But since you have used water and electricity from the guest house, you can pay what you like. No rules will be broken.'

Ishwari remembered the taxi driver from last night. Even he had left without taking the fare.

'It would be best if you leave before Nikhil returns,' he continued, unprompted.

'I realise you're helpless, Gourohori Babu,' she said. 'I met several helpless people yesterday. Some of them are famous, some impossibly rich. I was forced to appreciate each of their problems. So I do understand that an infirm, retired old man like you has no choice. I'm ready – take the keys, I'll pull the door shut when I go downstairs. What you have done for us is well beyond your means. Besides, there's no problem now. I'm sure I'll find a place to stay. But I am equally sure I won't find anyone as caring as you.'

'What is your name?'

'Ishwari.'

'Ishwari?' The old man's eyes glowed at the holiness of her name, even as anxiety suffused his brow. 'You're all alone, a woman, so young too. I have no idea where you've come from nor do I know how long you need to stay in a hotel with your child.'

The old man spoke deferentially, and she respected him for not asking any direct questions. 'This city is crammed with people, with houses and shops, buses and trams,' she said. 'There must be a room for us somewhere. I'm a healthy, capable adult – surely I will find work.'

'I am sure you will, but you will have to start from scratch.'

'So I shall. I have to. Roo and I were separated

from each other, it's only been three days since I've had him back. I'm not alone any more. I have a heavier burden now, my relationship with the world is stronger.'

'Roo is your own son, isn't he?' Gourohori said after some thought.

Ishwari laughed for the first time in three days. 'He is my son, Gourohori Babu, my very own. I gave birth to him.'

She went back to her room and folded her blanket, then got Roo dressed and returned with him. Gourohori Babu recommended a cheap guest house near Ballygunge Station. It was usually crowded by foreigners but it allowed people to stay for extended periods. 'There are many places where you can stay,' he told her, 'but you have to think of security first.'

She would actually have to stoop now, reflected Ishwari, and descent in this case meant degradation – degradation was her destiny. Ishwari walked along the passage with these thoughts running through her head while she balanced Roo and her luggage, and stopped abruptly when she heard an agitated voice coming from Gourohori Babu's room on her left. It couldn't be anyone but Nikhil Biswas. She sensed Gourohori Babu's apprehension as he said, 'Oh, no'.

I walk up to the door very slowly. The man with

a vengeful face standing in the middle of the room is about thirty-five. His expression is like an animal's. His chin protrudes well beyond his lips, jutting out like a fox's – he is dressed in jeans and a gaudy yellow T-shirt, white sports shoes on his feet. The face of a bully.

'Gourohori Babu?' I call out tentatively.

Inevitably, Nikhil Biswas begins to yelp. 'Are you the one who spent the night in the room on the terrace?'

'Yes.'

'I'm the manager here.'

'How wonderful – a pleasure to meet you.'

'Have the charges been discussed? Has the name been entered? Unaccompanied women are not allowed rooms here. This is what happens when senile old men run the show. They start thinking it's their family house, that they can do as they please.'

'Would you mind telling me what you mean?'

'Have you ever heard of a room on the roof being given out? Huh? We have important things stored there. I'll have to consider getting you out of here, Gourohori Babu. You're overstepping all limits!'

I cannot stand Nikhil Biswas's pointing finger, his body language. I find myself shaking with anger. I desperately want to start an argument with him. The concentrated mass of his invectives makes me want to retch. Nikhil Biswas's face merges instantly into the faces of the wealthy man, the legal expert, the bearded poet.

The poet had once told me, 'The poet's job is to take on the burden of the sorrows of the world on everyone's behalf!' He believes this statement of Baudelaire's, heart and soul. And it is from this credo that he has discovered the simplest way to bear this burden of sorrows. He has several overused words in his sling: burning, blazing, skull, socket, skeleton, torch, impoverished, master, rice, spoilt and so on. The sensibility, the purity of these words has long been blunted. But on the strength of these words he writes his poetry of protest, seated far from the flames with his newspaper and before his television. The flames do not singe him even a little but his face is radiant in their blazing glow. Those who have faith in him say that it is not possible to create art in this state of emergency – statements are sufficient in such a situation. They don't know that in a state of emergency what is needed is not art but humane behaviour, and that words have nothing to do with being humane. A nation that needs to be awakened through song, through poetry, has only emotion as its consciousness. Its sense of humane behaviour is that of a child's. As a result, the poet, the juggler of words, exploits human misery like any immoral political leader to fight for nothing but his own survival – and deceives everyone. He swindles them, he defrauds them. I know that he will conceal his shame at not letting a woman and her five-year-old son stay a single night in his house by forcing out a withered poem with constipated grunts and jerks, blaming his wife and her reign! He will be satisfied, and then make the rounds of literary associations and gatherings, reading his poem in his baritone to the accompaniment of sighs.

A suffering mother, a mother who wanders around the city with her child, will display deep respect for him, while he exits the gathering with stately steps, leaving behind an audience enthralled. As he embarks on that brief journey, he will think of himself as Socrates – a great philosopher who has survived two and a half millennia. And although most will not be able to do this, a handful of individuals will realise that no state of emergency will ever breathe life into his poetry again.

I plunge into an argument with Nikhil Biswas. By now Roo has slipped his hand out of mine and wandered off to the rabbit cage in one corner of the passage.

I confront Nikhil Biswas. 'So the roof is always

locked? Never used? Really?' Had the wealthy man or the poet or the legal expert given me shelter for a single night I might not have experienced this furious urge to cling to this space. 'Why don't you come upstairs with me right now – let me show you all the things I noticed on the terrace and in the bathroom and in the room on your roof. But we need to gather a couple of witnesses before that. Let people see what's actually going on here behind the façade of a guest house.'

The man falls silent suddenly like flames quenched by a jet of water, looking around in confusion and adjusting his collar. He does not display the courage to ask what I have seen. He doesn't wonder whether I really might know what's up there on the roof. After all, I have only occupied the room right on top. Gourohori had decided that the larger room on the roof was far too full of rubbish.

I cannot give Nikhil Biswas much time. 'Could you kindly tell me what the charge for the room is?' I ask.

'Five hundred,' he replies.

'Five hundred? What nonsense!' Gourohori exclaims.

'Yes, Dadu, five hundred.' Nikhil Biswas's eyes dance. 'You might have felt a surge of compassion late at night, but I focus on business, all right?'

Gourohori suddenly erupts. 'Shut up, you crook! Five hundred rupees is the regular room charge, Madam, don't pay a rupee more than two-fifty. The rest is between me and the owner.'

'You dare talk about the owner?' Nikhil screams.

Gourohori looks determined. 'Let me through,' he says, standing up, 'the child is running away.'

Two women and a man come down the stairs. Tamils. In English they begin to quiz Nikhil about where they can get idlis and dosas. Two or three people arrive simultaneously with their belongings in search of a room, so Nikhil is preoccupied.

'There's a south Indian restaurant across the road,' Gourohori tells me. 'Leave your luggage with me and have breakfast first.'

'He will take his revenge,' I tell him, 'and I won't be by your side then as you are by mine now.'

'What can he do,' answers Gourohori. 'I'm old, I've lived long enough. If a young woman like you with a child and nowhere to go isn't afraid, why should I be?'

It was eleven-thirty. What Roo needed was not south Indian food but a meal of rice, daal, butter and an egg. He desperately needed nutrition after two days of near starvation. The first thing Ishwari bought after leaving the guest house was a bottle of water. She also got two large bars of chocolate, two packets of biscuits and a slice of cake, and put them in her bag. She felt somewhat prepared now. Ishwari had realised yesterday that things like these were potent weapons in her battle for her child.

Ishwari crossed the road and climbed into a hand-drawn rickshaw. Roo was startled by the sight, just as he had been surprised at the sight of an Ambassador converted into a taxi. When she explained her requirement to the rickshaw-wala, he took a right turn, with the Dhakuria Lake to their left, and brought them to a restaurant, opposite a cinema hall, that served Bengali food.

The restaurant was small but tastefully furnished. Probably because it was just noon, the lunchtime crowd hadn't yet materialised. The smell of fish and meat being sautéed hung in the air. Scents like this forced the famished to forget all sense of etiquette and lick their lips and gulp hungrily.

As did Roo. Drawing his chair back to sit down, he smiled joyously at her. Settling him down, she tried on her part to ensure that they fulfilled each other's anxious expectations – even though Ishwari had turned her bag upside down to count all her money this morning and discovered that all calculations went haywire when times were bad.

Drawing the menu card towards herself, she asked Roo, 'Meat or fish? What'll it be? Chicken or mutton?' But she didn't hear his answer at all. Instead, she read the prices: Rs 295, Rs 350 + tax, packing charge: Rs 80.

It was so expensive! Ishwari was shocked.

Roo wanted to change his seat and sit down more comfortably, so that he could eat properly. She read the menu card carefully – the speciality of this restaurant lay in reviving centuries-old recipes with careful research. People could have lunch from the age of the Annadamangal or dinner from Phullara's banquets.

Ishwari could not work out a solution. And so, abandoning her self-respect in confusion, she swept up her son and left with him before the waiter's questioning eyes.

Such a retreat is a success in this novel of lies and truths – to the reader of this novel, I'm sure, all kinds of humiliation faced by humans, by the hungry, by the afflicted, by the beggar, by the injured, are effective. The more meticulous the description of this humiliation by a writer or poet or painter, the more successful they are, the more triumphant their art. The more the reader is bruised and upset after entering the novel, the more she considers the reading of it profitable. And so this cruelly predatory novel forced

Ishwari to race off, holding Roo by his injured hand, in the pursuit of a more hellish and demonic humiliation, while Roo kept saying with a desperation sharper than his pain, 'What's the matter, Ma? Aren't you eating? Aren't we eating? Ma? Ma…?'

Just as war, unrest and treachery are the capital of the weapon-manufacturing business, sterile humanity and its humiliation are the invaluable capital of literature. But creating this humiliation is agonizing. When I write that the novel written by a character named 'I' has been burnt to ashes, I want to weep. The first ten days, the memory of those pages grows stronger; a year later my relationship with what I wrote turns cold and hurt hovers over my living words. It raises a lament of grief. But the lines describing the midnight rattling of the gates of Dinratri remain just as much a record of 'events', just as much 'fact', just as 'practical' beneath the footsteps of time.

And just as true. As soon as this agony, this mortification sprang to mind, my novel turned as stiff and inflexible as the body does the moment it is penetrated by a syringe, and I pray in trepidation: oh god, must I churn the poison of this humiliation with my own hands in pursuit of my art? In other words (I'd have to write), Ishwari stopped running abruptly and Roo, panting and pale, extended his blue-veined hand from his shawl before Ishwari could construct an explanation, and said, 'The chocolate, then?'

I am defeated repeatedly by Roo's patience and endurance, and the desire for a tempestuous conflict rages within me. I rush back to Dinratri. If someone could occupy the attic for seven years, why can't Roo and I? Why can't we stay for a few days? I cannot abandon this city now. What I need is not a ramshackle room in a ladies' hostel or a paying guest's accommodation infested with cockroaches and lizards. I need this terrace.

Ishwari will occupy this room on the roof. The terrace is enormous, with mosaic tiles, sparkling white. The thick walls take several turns. They can easily play hide-and-seek in the darkness, she and Roo. And there's the brass tap running down the side of the huge water tank. She will do the dishes there, wash the clothes, spread them out to dry all over the roof and then dry her hair in the sun. Despite the lack of attention, how silky her auburn hair is. While Ishwari wanders, humming in the late afternoon, Roo will chase the tail of an insect.

Now and then, on the night of a new moon, when Roo slips into slumber, I will emerge from within Ishwari. Throttling myself, I will seek a gruesome resolution to all the things in my life that don't add up, but because I won't find one, I will pace up and down the roof, sobbing through my nose like an unloved witch. Even if it is through a conflict, I want this roof.

—

When Gourohori sees us he says, 'Have you eaten? Why so sad, young man? Haven't you eaten properly?'

'No, we couldn't eat,' I answer.

'Why not?'

'I'll come to that. First I need to talk to you about certain things.'

As we enter Dinratri, we see a young man standing near the gate, smoking. He begins to follow us in. I cannot bear the look in his eyes.

When I stop at Gourohori's door, the man pauses two steps behind me. I am forced to point him out to Gourohori. Looking grim, he says, 'What is it, Montu?'

Montu answers, 'Ashoke Da from Maharani was looking for you, he said there's some puja or something at the boss's house and that you'd be going, so you can go with him if you like.'

'I see,' says the old man. 'I don't know if I'm up to it. My foot aches constantly. Let's see, I'll let him know.'

'Hasn't this lady left yet?' Montu asks. 'Nikhil Da's

not very happy about this.'

'Oh, really?' says Gourohori.

'How come you're accepting guests without Nikhil Da's approval? Isn't it better to mind your own business at this age, Dadu?'

Gourohori suddenly began to cough violently. It was such a strong attack that Ishwari ran to get him a glass of water. Montu disappeared from the scene. I wait for his coughing to stop. I want to have the discussion as soon as he's recovered a little. There isn't much time and this is an experiment. If I am unsuccessful I have to find a hotel by evening. 'You said some people once lived in the room on the roof for seven years,' I say.

The old man immediately understands what I'm getting at. 'Oh no, how can that be possible!' he exclaims. 'There's been a change of ownership, this building now belongs to the second brother. He's a moody fellow, I'm not capable of explaining things to him.'

'I'll talk to him. I don't want to stay seven years, Gourohori Babu, only seven days, ten at most.'

'Can't be done, Madam. Impossible.'

'Nothing's impossible.'

'What have I got myself into? How did you come up with an idea like this?'

'There's a very good reason. It's a story. I don't want to tell you the story because it's no use. There's always a story, isn't there? The story might vary from one person to the next, but since last night, the course of the story has been the same for everyone. Even the options are identical, Gourohori Babu. Therefore, unable to find anyone to offer Roo and me a place to stay for the night, I came upon a guest house where not a single room was available. But I didn't have to go without a room. I was accommodated in the attic. And the story is at its strongest at this point. As an artist, am I not going to use it? But how? I have a little money. I can even get a job. But it will take time. Roo will have to go to school. Above all, I have to find some sort of place to stay. I have to make a beginning somewhere. All doors before me are closed and they may or may not open. My proposal has surprised you very much. But where's the harm in trying? The room on the roof would be good for me, for I have a child with me – how long can he be confined to a room? The roof will let us stretch our legs, and the bathroom's so far away the rent can't be high either. Now will the second brother agree to let me have it? And even if he does agree to give the room out, why to me? That's a closed door too, but it might open, mightn't it?'

—

Rantideb Mullick, the owner of Dinratri, the 'second son', was over sixty-five. In superb health, he oozed aristocracy. His hair was almost entirely grey, his eyes held a self-absorbed expression but were sharp nevertheless. Rantideb observed Ishwari and Roo closely as she told her story. As he listened, an entire cigarette burnt down to ash. On her way to Rantideb's house in Lovelock Place, Ishwari had learned that his family still owned twelve or thirteen buildings in the city. The building in which he lived was huge too. They had to cross an iron gate, gatekeepers and bulldogs to meet him. Gourohori had told her Rantideb was an engineer who had studied in England.

When Ishwari had made her proposal, Rantideb turned to Gourohori and said, 'Nikhil has become quite smart, hasn't he, Gourohori Babu?'

It was a strange question. The objective wasn't clear: did Rantideb want Nikhil to become smarter? Or was it a roundabout way of finding out what Nikhil was really up to?

'Nothing escapes your attention,' said Gourohori Babu.

'Hmm.' Rantideb nodded.

Ishwari had been led to a soft sofa. But Gourohori had been standing for nearly half an hour despite the pain in his leg. It is quite usual for an employee to remain standing before the owner but my mind begins to chafe with a desire to mediate. I say, 'Gouro-hori Babu was hurt in the leg a few days ago when he slipped and fell. May he sit down? He's been in a lot of trouble because of me since last night – I'm feeling terrible for him.'

'No, no, I'm fine,' Gourohori protests.

Rantideb transfers his steady eyes towards me before issuing an instruction in his unhurried man-ner: 'Sit down, Gourohori Babu.'

Gourohori leaves the room diffidently, returning with a stool. At this moment Roo raises his ankle to point it out to Rantideb. 'My foot hurts too.'

Frowning, Rantideb lowers his cigarette and leans forward. 'What's the matter?'

'I cut myself.'

'How?'

'Because I put on shoes without socks.'

(Roo is rambling. Let him.)

'You must put on your socks before your shoes.'

'I don't know how to put socks on.'

'Tell your mother.'

'She wasn't there. I had put on my best shoes because I was going to meet her. She was waiting for me far away.'

Rantideb fell silent. He had just returned from a game of golf. His towel was in his hand and he gave it to his servant. Then he said, 'In the process of becoming self-reliant, women in our country grow wayward most of the time. They forget principles and civility. Perhaps your sense of responsibility towards this child will prevent this eventuality. In any case, I am unable to come to a decision. But there is nothing wrong with your proposal. For now…' Ishwari couldn't breathe. '…for now, let her stay, Gourohori Babu. Let her have the roof. Shift whatever there is on the terrace to the garage. The garage is empty, I trust. I'm telephoning Nikhil. He will have the terrace and the toilet cleaned. Ishwari, you may use the attic as a kitchen.'

Gourohori was pleased. He rose to his feet, and Ishwari followed, saying, 'What about the room charges?'

'Just pay a hundred rupees a day. Clear the payment every three or four days. Gourohori Babu?'

'Sir?'

'See a doctor.'

Gourohori nodded, satisfied. Meanwhile, Ishwari could not believe she had been given the roof for a mere hundred rupees a day. This meant her philosophy was right – for every door that slammed on her face, another would be opened in welcome. Suddenly she felt relieved. Even after three days of wandering the streets, she was still unvanquished, wasn't she? Roo's hand was still in hers, wasn't it?

Ishwari's palms met each other in the traditional gesture of respect. 'Thank you so much,' she said.

Once outside, Ishwari realised Roo needed something to eat at once.

Before she left, Rantideb asked her if she would look for a job now. Ishwari nodded vehemently in response. Rantideb asked about her academic qualifications. She answered that although she had read science up to the university level, it was literature that she loved unreservedly. When Rantideb looked at her curiously, she told him a story, a story with watertight logic.

'Once, when I was seventeen or eighteen, for three days I was locked in a room in which all there was besides water to drink was books. Five or six books. I had no choice but to read during those three days – Joyce, Kafka, Eliot. As I read, I realised that literature was the only key that could help me escape from the locked room of life. Or, you could say, literature and art could take me beyond the limits of what this world, this universe, can offer me. People like me always want to escape the world, they want it very badly – and they choose art as their spaceship.'

Rantideb nodded in acquiescence, exclaiming, 'That's the right way to read! The situation in which you began to read was extremely symbolic, just right for the turnaround, just right to rebel. Do you think there can be a more artistic reason to start reading, Ishwari? I doubt it.' With a glint of amusement in his eyes, he continued, '"Rhapsody on a Windy Night" is one of my favourite poems. Have you read it?'

Ishwari looked at him with glittering, victorious eyes. 'She is alone / With all the old nocturnal smells / That cross and cross across her brain.'

Rantideb nodded approvingly, and repeated, pursing his lips, 'She is alone, she is alone.'

—

On the way back, Gourohori asks a strange question in the taxi. 'Are all the events in your life so terrifying and true?'

I answer, 'It is possible some of them are made up. But they cannot be said to be untrue, because if the logic in this story is watertight, it is bound to be true for certain characters in a certain space and time. Whether the 'I' who was standing before Rantideb Babu was me or not is also a riddle, isn't it, Gourohori Babu? Do you suppose I myself am aware of my reach?'

Because he understands none of this, the old man says, 'What I believe doesn't matter, that the owner understood is good enough.' I am about to speak further when Roo jumps into my lap and thrusts his head out of the window. His body twists and he heaves, his tiny frame shaking, and a stream of green and yellow water flows out of his mouth.

—

Roo recovered by evening. Gourohori tramped up the stairs again to bring him warm milk. Meanwhile, several incidents had occurred. Both Roo and Gouro-hori were taken to a doctor; concealing his surprise and annoyance, Nikhil Biswas had the roof cleaned; a table and a set of a chairs were added to go with the bed and cupboard in the room on the roof. Even if Ishwari only stayed two or three weeks, she would still have to cook, and she had begun to harbour dreams of using the attic as a kitchen, of cooking with fragrant spices by moonlight. Ishwari felt a thrill at the marvellous idea of trying out a brand-new recipe after climbing up the spiral staircase almost as far as outer space, picturing holding Roo in her lap and feeding him. And she sat on the iron staircase facing the evening, growing more and more amazed. Someone

seemed to be plastering a coat of red across the western sky. A cacophony of car horns floated up; in the
twilight the sounds were scattered, fragile, different
in a new way. This appeal that the city held for her –
someone who had returned but hadn't accomplished
her tasks here – this glow of love at dusk was tinged
with an unnatural pink. And since then she had been
reciting Eliot under her breath.

> The bed is open; the toothbrush hangs on the wall,
> Put your shoes at the door, sleep, prepare for life.

> The last twist of the knife.

If death came after this Ishwari was prepared to rebuff
it. She was a more powerful assassin than death itself
now.

Gourohori had become somewhat involved with
Roo. Perhaps his loneliness had made them more of
a novelty than a nuisance to each other. Right now
they were chatting. Let them – she would go out to
buy a sweater, clothes and sandals for Roo, along with
some essential food. 'If you can stay here with Roo
for a while, I'll go and do some quick shopping.'

The old man said, 'Lock the door to the roof. Else
I'll have to answer a thousand questions from Nikhil.

I'll sit here and tell Roo stories.'

'I'll be back before you know it,' Ishwari replied, endlessly grateful.

'I have a stove, you can use it,' said Gourohori, using the informal *tumi* with her for the first time.

She nodded. Roo said, 'Don't forget my toothbrush, Ma.'

Ishwari went through fifteen hundred rupees in no time. For Roo she got sandals, a sweater, two sets of clothes to wear at home, a pair of cotton shorts to go out in, and two T-shirts. Along with these, she bought enough rice, daal, cooking oil, salt, potatoes, onions, eggs, bread, butter, tea and sugar for a fortnight. A glass and a steel plate, bowls, spoons, a large pot, a bowl with a lid, a set of tea things, a mug, two thick cloth dusters and mosquito repellent. A toothbrush, baby cream, some drawing material and a notebook and pencil for Roo.

It was around seven when she returned to the guest house. As she was about to enter, a lanky young man appeared before her. He took the packets from her hands. Ishwari exclaimed, 'Why did you leave without taking your fare yesterday!'

Once again, his smile looks mysterious in the white light of the passage and the yellow glow from a nearby lamp-post. I realise this novel has no character at the moment like this young man, hence his desire to enter it. This narrative will now seek to emerge from the trappings of child and home and groceries to immerse itself in a physical relationship. It will seek love, or something complex, but this novel is one that rejects humanity, it is a story about discarding things. A novel of headlong descent into an overflowing crisis, of being pushed off the edge of a perilous precipice into the tranquil darkness of the ravine. Art riddled with ill-omens, worthy of its objective, driven by the arrogance, the vileness of Sakshi and Hitabrata. But though I consider the young taxi-driver mysterious, it is not my intention that this story should end with the trafficking of women. The disgrace I seek flows from human beings, and so...

The young man tilted his head and peered dimly at Ishwari in response to her question, and said, 'That's what I'm here for, to collect the fare.'

Ishwari realised he was lying. 'Then you'll have to take these up to the third floor,' she said.

'All right.'

'How did you know I was still here?'

The young man hesitated. 'I was dropping a passenger in the neighbourhood. I thought I'd ask the gentleman we met yesterday about you. I had a hunch that you'd get a room here in the morning.'

'Not just a room,' she laughed, 'I've got the entire roof.' She enjoyed being able to laugh easily. The muscles of her face were tired of being worried, troubled and miserable. 'That too at just a hundred rupees a day. Isn't that better than a cloistered room? Oh dear, I haven't even asked you your name.'

'Sukul. Sukul Das.'

'Sukul, can I make a demand of you?'

'Yes.' A touch of childishness tinged Sukul's pimpled cheeks.

'Do you know how to light a stove, Sukul? It's an old stove. Gourohori Babu has lent it to me. I have to cook for us now, but I don't know how to use a stove.'

'You'll be here for a few days, won't you?' said Sukul. 'I'll arrange for a portable gas cylinder for you. You can hire it.'

'Really? They can be hired?'

'Yes, an eighty-rupee refill lasts a long time, almost a fortnight.'

'Where do you live, Sukul?'

'Behind Kalighat. It's not a decent place, it's quite infamous.'

'Does your family live with you?'

They had reached the terrace. Ishwari unlocked the door and entered. Gourohori had switched on the light on the roof. The room was lit too. She saw

Roo sitting still on the bed and Gourohori dozing in the chair, surprised that Roo was so quiet and absent-minded. As she rushed into the room, she heard Sukul answer her last question, 'I don't really have a family to speak of.'

—

After Roo ate the boiled potato and fell asleep, Ishwari felt all her chores, all her alertness, end. Looking at Roo's sleeping face, she sighed. It was ten at night and bitterly cold, the noises outside had died down. Yesterday her head was buzzing with insecurity, the threat had diminished today and that was why the terrace wrapped in darkness appeared as vast as her melancholy, as unprotected as a void.

The trouble was the door leading out of the roof could not be locked from within, and this had become cause for worry. The bathroom was some distance away, she was afraid to use it at night because anyone could come up to the terrace – Nikhil Biswas or his cohorts. She had been given a large blanket in a white coverlet from Dinratri, and she had laid out her brown bedspread on the bed. Gourohori had lent her some cooking utensils and a few plates. She had already cleaned the room and put the dishes away.

As she sat on the bed and tucked her feet into

the blanket, she saw that Roo's eyebrows were furrowed. Perhaps he too was dreaming. What did either of them have now but dreams?

She would have to go out tomorrow morning and prepare her CV. There was a cyber-café close by. Ishwari tried to work out the contents in her head. She could meet some people she knew. But a wave of reluctance washed over her. She no longer wanted to depend on anyone she knew.

Pondering all this, she drifted off to sleep, and as Ishwari was snared in the cobwebs of her dreams, she imagined that Roo hadn't been born yet. He was still inside her womb. He was stirring, calling out to her apprehensively. But he didn't want to emerge, he didn't want to be separated from her, and he was swelling in size, his enlarged head was knocking about inside her. Ishwari was panting, she could not breathe, but she had no alternative but to bear her child's and her own undivided soul, emotions, demands and destiny – she couldn't do it, crumpling at the knees, she was knocked to the floor with her swollen belly.

—

Ishwari was shaken out of her slumber by the sound of the door to the terrace being opened – someone had come up to the roof. What time was it? She sensed someone prowling outside. Not one person, but two or three. She was afraid.

Her ears were pricked for another sound, her abdomen heavy. She desperately needed to urinate. She had never felt the urge so powerfully. It felt as though she would let go on the spot if she couldn't go to the bathroom at once. But how would she reach the bathroom now? She could risk neither her body nor her helpless child nor her money – who knew what dangers lurked outside? And the fault was hers, for why had she not noticed in the afternoon that the door was unlocked? Why, for that matter, had she hit the road with Roo? There is only one alternative – I have to forget this urge. I have to cast off this body. I have to control myself ruthlessly. Be ruthless enough to plug the hole. But how?

I do not know my future, but I know my past. I must move away from the present into that past and recollect a blow like a whiplash which I received, so that my mind and consciousness are numbed. I have to think of people like Sakshi and Hitabrata, or that child. The explosive room I was released into after marriage. And the ugly battle between my right and its denial. I have to think of the sperm devoid of love, which I did not want to accept and tried to block by stiffening the opening to my vagina and my entire body, like I am trying to do now. But because I couldn't, the product of the deceitful birth that ensued sleeps by my side now. But I do not hate him because I do not hate myself. Instead, I am optimistic about myself now, biased, the burnt novel is my life, I have to clear out the ashes and the toxic waste and give birth to new, cleansed letters. I am going to ask my novel what will bring it deliverance. Is it happiness or misery that this narrative seeks? Or will my creation reach the confluence of genuine happiness and unredeemed misery?

Am I then actually capable of considering happiness at this moment of doubt instead of thinking only of a lifetime of defeat? Dare I imagine that the power of such happiness is no less than that of misery? Happiness, love, transcendence – will these become my themes in the end?

I used to own a pair of black capri pants. Women in this city didn't normally wear such clothes in those days. One morning I dressed sleepily for college and chose the capri pants, but I hadn't noticed a reddish streak running down the exposed portion of my right leg – it was a line of blood mingled with water that had trickled down from my thigh and dried. I was on my period, that's what happens to women: the blood trickles down in the gap between one sanitary pad and the next.

I took my seat in an auto-rickshaw in this state, and what I had not noticed attracted the attention of a young man sitting next to me. Following his eyes, I saw the red streak and felt embarrassed. Unable to tear his eyes away, he stared at me unabashedly. Suddenly he asked, 'Did you cut yourself?'

'No,' I answered.

He understood nothing at first, then his expression changed. 'Need help?' he asked.

Our journey ended at this point. He continued walking by my side as though in a trance. As though he understood that what he had seen was not usually visible. Not just the body of a woman, this was more than that – it was like witnessing an establishment of womanhood.

Still walking, we came up to a tree and it began to rain torrentially. It was the kind of rain that obliterates the earth. The young man suddenly brought a white handkerchief out of his pocket, moistened it in the rain and, kneeling on the ground, cleaned the red streak with great care.

We were two drenched individuals. A heavenly glow lit up his face. I emerged from the canopy of the tree, a water-nymph, joy bursting within me like colours inside a kaleidoscope. The colour of the cloudy

day was Picasso's yellow. Jerked out of my life of con-
tempt, derision and abuse, I began to walk. I took his
hand. And I fell in love for the first time.

This love was greater than all the meaninglessness,
all the disgrace in my life. It was divine. Springing
to life through the merits of existence, from pallid to
vivacious, I felt animated. This love, its whirling circle
enveloping me with its unselfish touch, did exist once.
Once? But not any more? Oh, oh, oh – was there
happiness once, striking back at misery? You cannot
believe it at this hour of night amid such fear and
insecurity, can you, Ishwari? There is no one today,
but still your memory won't fade, like the symptom
of a disease that will never leave you. Is there no love
any more, does no one want you any more? Answer,
Ishwari. Come out of the story and answer, break the
false pomp and ceremony of literature and tell the
truth, Ishwari. Answer now, aren't you still looking
for someone to give yourself to? Answer, and let your
mind abandon your body, tremble like a reed in the
wind and do not notice when, breaking through all
resistance, your urine escapes your body, soaking your
clothes, wetting the floor, touching the water bottle, Roo's shoes and the other things lying about, and
flows away slowly, like an unhurried deluge. You do
not even realise.

—

This is an imagined battle that has taken root within me. Handing Roo over to Gourohori, to Sukul, I have devoted myself, heart and soul, to gathering the principal weapon for my battle. Gourohori has no family, Sukul has no family; this has worked to my advantage. Because I have accepted Sukul easily, he has become my mainstay for all my minor requirements. He visits every morning and evening. He doesn't smile, doesn't say much, but honours each of my requests. I get a job but I might as well not have one. I work for an NGO for five days. My job is to talk on the phone – to talk to people who are about to commit suicide and in the process temporarily put to sleep their desire to kill themselves. Bring them back from the brink of danger, so to speak.

For five days I speak for six hours continuously on the suicide helpline as though I am in a trance. From three in the morning to nine, when the rest of the city is stirring. Apparently society is at its most suicidal when night turns into day. Locking the sleeping Roo in the room during these six hours, an Ishwari whose grief has receded, an Ishwari without the seeds of a suicide wish, babbled continuously with several dangerously dark characters. A few days later she realised her body reeked of suicide. One day, instead of dissuading the caller from committing suicide, she said lucidly, yes, this is the solution: Valium, a dagger, a hammer, a blade, a nylon rope, acid, petrol, diesel, insecticide... all of these are acceptable solutions. The caller listened in silence, then disconnected.

I lose my job the next day. When I return home and take a bath, I feel like a rubber tree that yields a thick sticky sap of suicide as soon as its bark is sliced.

—

When Ishwari went to work, she wished Roo would remain asleep, that he wouldn't wake up. But Ishwari realised from the way Roo stared at her in the morning with disbelieving eyes, ignoring the blinding daylight, that he had woken up and sat up in bed while it was still dark, had groped for her, called her, been too scared to get out of bed, and had ended up urinating on the mattress. When I see the wet bed, I slap him. I tell him, 'Don't be disobedient, haven't I taught you what to do?'

The next day I discover a drain at the bottom of one of the walls. Although Sukul has arranged for a padlock so that we can lock the door leading downstairs from the roof, we stop visiting the bathroom at night. We don't like the terrace at that hour. Even after she quit her job with the NGO, Ishwari kept wishing Roo would remain asleep, that he would spend most of his time asleep. She went to the market, to the post-office, went for walk-in interviews, sometimes the road to an unplanned trip beckoned to her in the dim moonlight, but she could not extricate herself because of Roo – and then she wanted Roo to fall asleep. I hold his limbs down, thumping him thumping him. I thump him, thump him, thump him till he dissolves in the bed.

'My whole body hurts, Ma,' says Roo. 'Let me go, Ma. I'll go to sleep.'

Ishwari didn't last more than five days at her second job either. On her fifth day of work at an event management company in Salt Lake, Roo fell severely ill. For three out of the five days, Roo had been locked in the room from nine in the morning to seven in the evening. When he threw up on the fourth day, Ishwari requested Sukul to stay with Roo. Gourohori stayed by his side on the fifth day – that night Roo began to burn with a high fever. He had to be taken to the doctor. The doctor said Roo had had a terrible fright for some reason. On the sixth day she quit her job. On the eighth morning, after she had spent two days with her son in her lap, a smile as light as a feather appeared at the corners of Roo's mouth. She gave her son a cup of tea. Bringing the cup to his lips, Roo began to blow mightily on it. And she saw that though her Mahiruho was smiling, he had dark circles under his eyes. It seemed the disease would gradually manifest itself through additional symptoms of uncertainty. And Ishwari's imagined struggle would become even more substantial.

And as Ishwari fed her son bread and butter, as she cooled the rice with boiled potatoes and boiled eggs, as she washed her clothes, as she paid Nikhil Biswas three hundred rupees every three days, as she felt heartfelt gratitude for Sukul and Gourohori for the smallest of reasons, she pondered, holding a head made incredibly heavy with despair, 'What now? After this, what?' As she wondered, she found her third job: the post of warden at the girls' hostel of a boarding school that had come up on the outskirts of Calcutta. She got the job almost miraculously. She met the authorities and explained her situation to them, including Roo's condition, and in exchange for her entire salary her son received permission to join the school and the hostel. Ishwari wept without restrain that day – weeping by herself, clutching her head – thanking providence that at least she and Roo had not had to let go of each other's firmly held hands and be catapulted into the distance, where they might as well not have existed.

Gourohori had tears of happiness in his eyes when he heard this news. Sukul continued to look at her and her child with cool eyes. 'This is a good option,' he said. Even Nikhil Biswas told me as he tucked the three notes into the drawer, 'Finally something's worked out for you. When are you moving? I'll let Mr Mullick know.'

I am enraged by this, for Nikhil Biswas has long been awaiting my departure. Because of the lock on the terrace door, Nikhil Biswas has been forced to put an end to his nocturnal drinking sessions with Montu, Prabir and several other scroungers in the neighbour-hood. My presence had also prevented Nikhil Biswas from continuing the unhealthy practices that lurk in the rooms of Dinratri. When I step onto the terrace for a breath of fresh air in the evening, I sometimes see a couple or a middle-aged man and a young woman arrive on a bike or in a car, and leave in just a few minutes. This movement, signalling disappointment and thwarted lust, does not escape Gourohori's atten-tion either.

On the day Ishwari was due to start her new job, the day she was to leave Dinratri with Roo – which was why the two were bathed and dressed early in the morning, Sukul having arrived to take them in his taxi, while Gourohori had overcome his aching foot to come up to the terrace to help Ishwari – there was a phone call for her in Nikhil Biswas's office.

A phone call? For her? Ishwari turned cold with fear. She had been waiting for this phone call for a long time, or apprehending something equally dangerous. She was terrorised by the thought that Roo would eventually be snatched away from her. No one here knows she is on the run with Roo. Only I know – and the poet, the rich man and the lawyer know. Now Ishwari concluded that Roo's claimants had tracked her down. And they were coming to take Roo away from her. Ishwari went downstairs slowly, dragging her feet. Her senses were in agony. She would have to give Roo up – she would have no choice – for she had legally relinquished her rights over Roo, abandoned him – eight, no, nine months ago.

Nikhil Biswas's presence was invisible amidst her silent wails as she pressed the receiver to her ear and said in a trembling voice, 'Hello?'

An impossibly dignified voice said at the other end, 'Hello. This is Rantideb Mullick. I believe you're leaving today.' Overwhelmed, she murmured, 'Yes.'

'I'm extremely relieved about this job of yours. A solution could not have been possible unless the almighty had willed it. Don't you agree?'

'It must be so, Mr Mullick,' she answered softly.

'Are you leaving right away?'

'Yes,' she said. 'I have a request, Rantideb Babu.'
Even a minute ago she hadn't thought of saying this.

'Yes?'

'May I keep the room for two more days?'

'Yes, you may, but might I ask why?'

'I cannot say for certain but something tells me I'll
have to come back here.'

Rantideb said, 'That doesn't sound good. Are you
worried the place won't suit you?'

'I can't quite explain it. I keep thinking I'll be
helpless the moment I leave the terrace. I won't have
anything or anyone to call my own. This sanctuary is
the last place on earth for me.'

It was evident once more that Rantideb Mullick
was a man of few words. 'Why don't you go along
now. I'm informing Nikhil, he will give you the key.'

Leaving everything else behind, and carrying
clothes for only five days, Ishwari left Dinratri with
Sukul, holding Roo's hand.

—

Sukul went back after dropping her to the sprawling
campus of the school. He refused the taxi-fare. He
hugged Roo in silence, cast frozen eyes on Ishwari,

and then departed, leaving behind a trail of smoke. 'I'm going,' he said as he left. Sukul's mother was dead, his father was dead, he had no brothers or sisters. In spite of this, no form of address had been established in their relationship. No 'Didi' nor 'Madam' or anything like that – Sukul was an uneducated male, she was an educated woman, the relationship between them had developed precisely as these circumstances decreed, though she was now unilaterally dependent on him. She even left Roo in his taxi when she went into shops to buy things.

The school authorities had asked her to meet them in the first instances, fill in her joining report and then complete the formalities of having Roo admitted to the school and to the boys' hostel. Asking her son to wait on the bench outside the office, Ishwari entered the principal's chamber. Her name was Rani Seth – with an effusive smile she offered Ishwari a seat. 'Would you like some tea or coffee?' she asked.

'No, thank you.'

'So, all well?'

'Yes, Mrs Seth.'

'Is your son here with you?'

'Yes, Madam.'

'We are happy to have found someone like you, Ishwari.' Ishwari looked at Rani Seth with wide eyes.

'Look, it's very difficult to find someone educated, young, and at the same time without anyone or anything holding them back. You are all of these in one person.'

'But I do have someone holding me back,' she responded. 'I have a son.'

'But he won't hold you back any more, will he? He'll practically be living with you. The girls' hostel and boys' hostel face each other.'

'I'm lucky,' she said.

'Indeed, you are. You're lucky, so are we.'

'I could only have dreamt of such an arrangement. I want to thank you, Mrs Seth. A thousand times.'

'Enough, Ishwari. You still have to complete the formalities – please take care of these first, we'll talk again later. Sign your joining letter. Go to the office after that – you'll find Ashwini Dutta over there, she'll prepare your child's papers. Just fill out the form and give her your son's original birth certificate, she'll photocopy it and return the original document to you.'

'Birth certificate?'

'Yes, birth certificate.'

'I don't have his birth certificate.'

'You mean you aren't carrying it?' Rani Seth's eyes narrowed.

'I mean I never had it.'

Mrs Seth let herself fall back into her large revolving chair. 'Then arrange for it. It's a necessity. Your son won't be admitted without a birth certificate, Ishwari.'

'It's practically impossible to get hold of, Mrs Seth.'

'What can we do? We can't change the system. There are certain norms. They cannot be changed for one individual.'

'You must do something, please.' Her words spun about in the air-conditioned chamber. 'Please.'

'There's nothing I can do. The authorities won't accept it. How do I know this child is yours? Where's the proof?'

'He is my child, Mrs Seth, my own child. Believe me. I tore myself apart to give birth to him. Look at his features, they're just like mine. Look at the way we exchange glances.'

'Ishwari, you can have your job, but as far as your child is concerned, I'm helpless. Just bring the certificate and make use of the opportunity we're providing you so considerately.'

Ishwari wanted to scream. 'And if I can't, is his education going to come to an end? Will he never get a chance to study in a school? He's been born – does that need to be proved? He's a human being – does that need to be proved? Education is his right no matter what his date of birth or the identity of his parents. Why can't he be admitted?'

'Society follows certain rules, Ishwari. They're tried and tested.'

'Do you know, Mrs Seth, that I didn't have a birth certificate either, at first? An imaginary birthday was assigned to me on the basis of the movement of my eyes, the strength of my cries, the power with which I sucked milk. Still I survived.' Ishwari brought her fist down on the desk.

'Oh my god! This is too much now. You will break this glass!'

'I know there are no miracles in life. But Mrs Seth, if I must break, I will break alone.'

—

Rantideb Mullick had invited Eliot into her mind. All over again. On her way back to Dinratri from Rani Seth's sprawling kingdom, she kept muttering Eliot like someone who was pursued by a nightmare.

I climb up to the terrace. I give Rantideb a half-truth as my reason for returning to the guest house. He doesn't ask any questions. Once again Roo begins to spend his days locked up in the room. Sukul's eyes are so deeply disturbed when he sees us that they are better described as anguished.

I start looking for another job. I no longer wish to link my blemished fate, my reserve or my integrity to employment. I begin to look for the kind of neutral work that will be sought after and performed by my body while my mind remains insulated, preserved for the purpose of writing a lacklustre, sober, nameless, meandering novel.

Thus fusing philosophy with employment, I try to lighten the burden on my heart. Meanwhile Roo develops a fever: high temperature, vomiting, stomach ache. A day passes and it does not cease. I try to save money, and wait for Roo to get better on his own. Wondering why he throws up despite being on a diet of just daal, rice and boiled potato, I grow irritated. Roo recovers two days later. Ishwari pulled his eyes down to take a look at the whites – yes, they seemed less bloodshot.

Four or five days later, the fever, vomiting and stomach ache begin again. I take a decision. I remove eggs from his diet, then milk. Famished, the boy chews his rice. Roo's face shrinks, only his unresisting eyes are visible. I count my money to see if I have enough for the doctor's fees, and suddenly winter abandons the city. Still Roo floods the room with his vomit. He talks far less now.

—

A little boy runs to his mother and she enfolds him in her embrace. Selling her body and pawning her soul, she makes him her anchor and survives. She spends sleepless nights over his illness, loses all her beauty as she stays awake night after night, and though it gasps for breath, her never-ending love continues to float like a tiny boat on an enormous ocean.

Disengaging himself from such tales, the child in this novel – this predatory novel – the child with eyes like a deer caught in the headlights, pleads, 'Can I sit in your lap, Ma?'

And his mother moves away. She locks him into the room and leaves because she feels that the child's head is too heavy, her thighs ache when he puts his head in her lap – she is unable to bear the burden of this head, of this child – so she rejects him, pushes him away, and meanwhile his fever climbs. As his temperature rises the boy is swept away like crude debris in a flood – he babbles in delirium. Within this delirium a mother's love and a guardian's failure groan mutely, suffering continuously. As I try to write this novel, I only want to escape this self-torture and go where there's nothing but the sea and Roo and me. Where we will see no ship on the crest of a wave, but where Roo and I will be born until we die amidst our mutual love and hurt – we will be born again and again. In this way mother and child will live in each other's lifespans till they die and still our destiny will not succeed in separating us.

But who would sacrifice this city, this hyper-reality, the right to this symbolic metropolis, and go off to the untrammelled beach? What will happen to this novel then? To all novels? What will happen to the meanness, the hard-heartedness, the shamelessness of literature? Most importantly, what will happen to the thirst for ultimate degradation, for the abstract, deformed metaphor of humiliation? Therefore neither Ishwari nor I will escape anywhere with Roo. This narrative will continue to shriek as its characters claw their way between the poles of extreme humanity and extreme art.

Ishwari is not what I am.

So the sun is shining formidably, and the big flamboyant poinciana and myrtle trees are bursting with red and yellow and violet flowers all the way from the crossroads of Rashbehari Avenue and Lansdowne Road down to Dhakuria Lake. And unbelievably, a blooming bough of forest flame is peeping over the wall of Ishwari's roof.

With the sun lighting up the red flowers falling

by her shoulder, Ishwari counted the days until her money would run out. Roo was sprawled on the spotless floor of the terrace with his drawing book and colour pencils. He had been better for the past five days. Ishwari was wondering whether to give him some stewed apple to eat. Roo couldn't eat green vegetables or fruit. He threw up at once. The boy had turned pallid. Stewing the apple a little would increase its iron content just as boiling a potato increases the amount of vitamin C in it.

With these ideas running through her head, Ishwari shook the last grains of rice out of the packet and put it in the pot. Then she spread out the last three days' newspapers on the bed. Two or three of the jobs advertised looked suitable. She sat down on the windowsill on the eastern wall, folding her legs beneath her. Three of the walls in this room had windows, each of them with large windowsills that were comfortable to sit on. She watched the sky turn blue-gold. The air seemed golden too, giving her goosepimples. What a beautiful day.

Beyond the perimeter of Dinratri was a bylane and on its other side a very high wall. Behind the wall was a house. From her window Ishwari could see right into it. There was always a bustle on the ground floor of the house, the first floor was relatively tranquil. The courtyard was paved with marble. There was an area for washing beneath a tap, lined with papaya trees. A veranda ran around the first floor, ornamental lattice work adorning its railing, and two rooms opened out into the exterior space. When the tall wooden doors were open, Ishwari had a view of the rooms within. There were plants in the veranda too.

Over the past month and a half, Ishwari had been observing the daily goings-on inside this house. Today it seemed more silent than usual. Only a low voice or two could be heard, if at all. Finding the left-hand door wide open, Ishwari forgot herself and stared inside the room. She forgot the rice on the stove. She even forgot Roo.

Years of organised and disciplined domesticity were evident everywhere. Shadows rested everywhere, the floors were cool and quiet and slick. The frills at the edges of the curtains and the cut of the perfectly crimped pillowcases were flawless, the bed was neatly made, the white bedclothes were stainless. The furniture was impeccably polished: an ancient dresser with rows of drawers and a circular mirror stood on slim serrated legs; next to it was a circular mahogany clothes stand, on it were draped stacks of white petticoats and white saris with red borders. The petticoats were old-fashioned, a single glance was enough to tell

that they belonged to a plump, aged, loving Bengali
wife – her husband, inevitably, was at the helm of this
household. The busy individuals on the ground floor
followed her orders – it was on her instructions that a
torrent of people flowed from one end of the house
to the other. It was on these instructions that the glass
doors and windows were being wiped and polished,
that those who came to the house seeking alms were
being fed.

As she gazed at these everyday scenes, Ishwari suddenly felt pained. She wanted to run to the old lady
and ask: how many years have you been here, at this
spot? How long have you spent as part of this room,
this house, this household? How many years has it
been since change crossed your threshold, how long
since the currents of time stopped? Has no one ever
asked you to go away? Have you never had to run
from one home to another? Has the infamy of broken
relationships never pursued you down dirty avenues?
Have you never sat on the pavement and wept? Have
hunger and thirst never melted the truth as hard as
metal, the resolve as unshakeable as rock within you?
Has your serenity, love, friendliness, behaviour or
courtesy never been made to plunge into the currents
of hell? When did you come to the conclusion that
this is your life – that, like the fixed existence within

the circuits of the cut-glass bulbs that light up every home at six in the evening, this is the ultimate form, the final shape, that this will never change? When did you realise this? Or can you break away yet? Or does fear creep down your spine like a snake, lurking under your bed, poised to grip your feet whenever you dangle your legs over the side?

I am jolted back to reality – Roo appears before me. He holds out his drawing book, he has drawn a picture, it's badly done. He has drawn me. I can't see myself in the picture. I think he is secretly demanding food.

—

Whenever I wander to that particular side of the terrace, a life I've always dreamed of materialises in all its finery. Their milkman gradually becomes familiar to me. I know what time their day begins, whom the room on the right belongs to, which days of the week he comes home. I am happy when he does. He smokes at night in this southern veranda, the glow of the cigarette singes my soul through the gaps in the papaya leaves, and my body turns restless. I am reminded how long it has been since my body has joined another. The instant I think this, my conflict with myself bursts into flame. I run outside to the terrace, bemoaning my existence, smiting myself on the breast – why couldn't I have been one of them? Or like them? Like these people? My arid emotions seek an answer.

Roo coughs in his sleep, he coughs all night. I pay no attention. I lean over the wall, looking in the direction of Lansdowne Road.

Lansdowne Road by night is very different from Lansdowne Road by day – that's when you see how many poor people there are in this rich neighbourhood. As night deepens and cars are tucked into parking spaces bought at three thousand rupees per square foot, beggars seek sleep and other journeys into oblivion.

On the days that the most lethal questions about her life occurred to Ishwari, she came to the other part of the terrace. And she confused her own existence for those of the beggars. Her identity seemed to emerge in response to the irresistible call of the nocturnal spirit that preys on human souls. Her self-confidence, found wanting, went to sleep in a dirty, tattered sari under the portico of the Hanuman temple with her head on her arm. An emaciated child slept next to her like a bundle of cloth. This child had no identity worth revealing to society. For she herself didn't know who the child's father was. She slept here, an anonymous stranger woke her up every night. She didn't rub her eyes as she sat up, didn't even bother to open her eyes completely – reluctant as she was to snap fully out of sleep. She rose to her feet and lay down behind the pillar on her back, lifting her sari up to her waist. Loosening her floppy blouse, kept in place with a safety-pin, she released one of the means of sexual enjoyment. High on country liquor, the disturbed old man – or perhaps he was young, depending on who it was on any given day – attacked her pure, flesh-and-blood body (bodies are always pure) like a beast, or threw himself on her and wept. Parting her legs, she put her hands beneath her head and snatched a few seconds of sleep in the intervals. If any of them overdid their ardour, taking too much time or nipping and biting unnecessarily, she either shook him off or issued a listless instruction to whoever was sleeping nearby: 'Get this bastard off me, will you'. If it turned out to be a powerful brute, she urged him, 'Why don't you fuck your mother?'

She swore mildly, and someone came over to mediate between her and her customer. On her part, she said, 'Let me go, not tonight, come tomorrow,' in a way that ensured sleep didn't desert her completely. Night after night passed in this way. An unending supply of unending sperm conducted victory marches into her uterus. Sometimes her elbows were grazed and her knees scratched by the concrete – she heaped curses on some unknown person, sobbed loudly, but, like Ishwari, she was never willing to reject the bundle that was her child. She could not even imagine such a thing. Whatever she got each night was what she got all her life. This child, this sex, these twenty rupees, this pavement, this pink portico, the myrtle blossoms in the storm, the clouds and the rain. She did not expect any of this. But each of them came to her of its own volition. She did not refuse anything that was given to her this way.

One day her advanced age was discovered, her skin was wrinkled. Her breasts and thighs sagged, her waist collapsed. And still, like the truth in this novel, like the truth in its lies, like the undistorted truth, someone or the other woke her up. Perhaps she was paid only five or ten rupees now.

When Ishwari of the pavement fell asleep, Ishwari of the terrace returned to the room where her ailing, starving child lay. He had turned skinny and emaciated in just a few days, but still his dreamy eyes stood out like clusters of flowers amid sunken cheeks and a bulging forehead. As she returned, Ishwari felt her life on the roof drag itself on its stomach along the length of the days between the house behind the wall on one side and the pavement on the other.

—

Ishwari had run out of money. For the past two days, Roo had been ill. A few days earlier she had discovered that Roo could not keep vegetables down in any form – raw or cooked. He began to throw up as soon as he ate. The day before yesterday, she had taken Roo to the doctor. Having spent three hundred rupees for the room at Dinratri, Ishwari was penniless. The doctor gave instructions for an ultrasound examination. He asked for milk, eggs, fruit and vegetables to be withdrawn from Roo's diet. Roo was forbidden everything except starchy rice and fresh fish. But the doctor was silent about just what Roo's illness was. Ishwari thanked my meanness this time. I stopped milk and eggs fifteen days ago. Just as well, or Roo's condition would have worsened. Both milk and eggs are poisonous for Roo now, poison for Ishwari's Mahiruho.

Roo has a fever. But since there is nothing else to do but pour water on his head, I go up to the window to the north and sit down. 'He' has been here since yesterday. He came last evening. Roo was throwing up violently at the time, through his mouth and nose. My arteries and veins were clogged with a depression as dense as smoke. I didn't want to get up and clean the vomit. Instead, I wanted to talk, to say things I cannot say to Sukul or to Gourohori: that I've run out of money, that my son is ill, that I don't have a job, that I am getting a job but I cannot settle down while Roo is sinking, that Roo is forgetting how to read and write... Besides these, there are other things to say too, buried deep inside – things about being enraptured, about blunders, madness, intoxication – I want to tell someone all these things. I told Sukul to call one of those street vendors who trade in shawls – it is time to sell my valuable shahtoosh. Sukul made enquiries and informed me that no vendor could afford to buy a genuine shahtoosh. A few days later he brought word of a shawl-collector in Mudiali. Ishwari took the shawl one evening to his small museum. He examined it at length, and then said with a smile, 'This isn't shahtoosh.'

'Not shahtoosh?' Ishwari shot upright. I am speechless too. 'What are you saying? It isn't shahtoosh?' We retreated a couple of steps, two astonished women. 'Not shahtoosh?' I say, indignation in my voice. 'Not shahtoosh?' Ishwari wailed in despair.

'No, it's not,' replied the collector. 'If it had been shahtoosh this four by six feet shawl would have weighed just fifty grams, but this one's over a hundred.' He rose to his feet.

Ishwari groaned and went out. She sank down beneath a tree. 'Not shahtoosh? Isn't shahtoosh shahtoosh, isn't truth the truth? Aren't any of the things I thought of all my life as art, as shahtoosh, as deliverance, as prayer, real? Not art? Not shahtoosh?' Her eyes bloodshot, she said, 'Roo's attempt to survive by winding himself around me is as worthless as the shawl. As dishonourable as the shahtoosh.'

Montu appears at my door. After a glance at the vomit all over the floor and then at Roo, he says, 'There's a phone call for you.'

I run downstairs. I couldn't pay the rent yesterday. I haven't paid the rent for four days now, why should Nikhil wait any longer? Rantideb has come to know and that's why he is telephoning. Will he tell me to leave? If he does, what reason shall I cite for letting me stay? Over the past month and a half, I have accepted Rantideb's help but not his charity – the moment I articulate my inability to pay, I will become a beggar in his eyes, my dignity will be ground to dust in the twinkling of an eye. Who will save me now?

'Were you busy?' Rantideb's voice broke into the receiver.

'Busy? I have nothing to be busy with.' Tears streamed from Ishwari's eyes like a jug of water suddenly overturned by a careless wave of the hand.

'Is the child well?'

'No, he's not.'

'Have you consulted a doctor?'

'Yes, yesterday.'

'Did he say what's wrong?'

'No. He's asked for an ultrasound, blood and stool tests.'

'Any job offers yet?'

'None.'

'There's a job going. You could try it out, you'll enjoy it.'

The bankrupt, stricken Ishwari said, 'I thought you were telephoning to tell me to leave. I owe you four days' rent, Mr Mullick. But I don't have a penny on me right now.'

After a brief pause, Rantideb said, 'The work may seem strange to you but it is not undignified. The son of a close friend of mine has had several successive tragedies in his life, Ishwari. About a year ago, Biba-swan's wife Tania died in childbirth, along with the baby. Before he could recover from the grief, Bubu had a terrible accident in Mumbai a few months ago. Not only was he grievously injured, a woman and her child were knocked down by his car and killed. Bubu was in America for treatment for about six months.

He was brought back to Calcutta just a few days ago. He hasn't recovered fully yet. And more importantly, he hasn't recovered from the trauma. Bubu is by nature an art lover, a little oversensitive, he doesn't get along with too many people. And now that he's ill, he's become particularly lonely. His mother is busy – she's involved with various things, his father even more so. His sisters live outside Calcutta. He has no one to talk to, no one with whom he can share the things he loves – music, books, paintings. He needs a like-minded companion, someone who will cheer him up and see that he doesn't wallow in his own loneliness. We have been trying to figure out what to do. We even advertised for a position, but he didn't like any of the candidates who came in for an interview.

'Then I happened to think of you, Ishwari. And I insisted you were the right person. I gave him some details about you. I told Bibaswan, Ishwari hates Mumbai too, just like you. What they'll offer you for this work is quite a large sum of money, Ishwari. Even after paying your rent at Dinratri and appointing a full-time maid, you'll have six or seven thousand rupees left over. You need money, Ishwari. Mahiruho needs proper treatment. It will take Bibaswan four months to recover completely. I hope your child will be better by then. So I suggest you think it over, and let me know what you decide. I'll telephone you again tomorrow.'

'There's nothing to think over, Mr Mullick,' she replied. Her tears had stopped. 'You know very well that I cannot dream of a better opportunity right now.'

'I'm glad, Ishwari. You're going to work with a very influential family, it will serve you in good stead. And they are good people. The kind of good people who know how to value qualities and abilities when they see them in others.'

Replacing the receiver, Ishwari raced off to Gourohori, who was sorting out his aluminium trunk. Startled, he asked, 'How's Roo?'

'I'm tired of addressing you formally, Gourohori Babu!' she replied.

—

Rantideb sent his car at about three-thirty on Sunday – the driver had been instructed to take Ishwari to Radheshyam House in Hastings. Rantideb had told the family she would be coming then. He had wanted to do the introductions himself, but he had to leave for Delhi the same day to fight a property case in the Supreme Court. So Ishwari would have to perform her own introductions.

Since it was Sunday, one could only hope that every member of Radheshyam House would be present. If they approved of Ishwari and she of them, she would gain the right to frequent every corner of the house, so that everyone in the household would know who she was and vice versa. It was almost time – Ishwari was all dressed up and waiting for the car.

She possessed just one sari: coarse, handwoven, saffron in colour, with a border the shade of earth. And she owned a single blouse: white, sleeveless, high-necked. She had dressed in these two items of clothing with great care, pinning the loose end of the sari to her shoulder. The sari was shorter than usual, and the end barely covered her back as she draped it around herself. She had brushed her hair and tied it back in a loose bun. She had only one perfume: Anais, from way back when. She had applied miserly dabs of it on her pulse points. When she was ready, she had hugged Roo and asked him, 'Does it work?'

Roo raised tired eyes from his rice and boiled potato. 'It does.'

The boy was so cold to the touch that Ishwari felt it would not be right to leave him alone and go anywhere today. I restrain Ishwari – as soon as Sukul arrives I say goodbye to Roo and go downstairs swiftly, telling the driver, 'Let's go.'

And then we move. Only I can hear the buzz of crickets in the air. My authentic self is imprinted in my brain, exposed only to me. The Ishwari that Rantideb knows of, that Sukul and Gourohori Babu know of, is only a story. This is the self which needs to be presented at Radheshyam House. But I have seen my novel burn down before my eyes. Shouldn't I want my story to change? As long as every character's true identity does not light up like phosphorus, the story can change over and over again. A person who can ask herself 'Why am I what I am?' and receive an answer is capable of creating a new narrative at every sunset. Just as I have made the real narrative of this novel as palpable as a bullet wound. The name of that wound is Roo. Mahiruho. Am I or am I not progressing towards literary achievement with Roo? Suddenly I realise just who Roo is in this predatory novel – he is the last supper at the hour of death by the swamp.

Rantideb's car is well-known here. The security guard opens the black iron gates as soon as the car blows its horn. Bibaswan's father Budhaditya Bagchi, who is Rantideb's friend, is one of the country's most eminent criminal lawyers. No one knows where he will be at any given point, but wherever he is, he is accompanied by his personal bodyguard. Security is of concern at his residence too, security for his wife and children. Budhaditya Bagchi is fighting the murder case of a Member of Parliament from the petroleum ministry, and has become a thorn in the side of several mafia groups.

The Bagchi family is rather concerned with security at Radheshyam House. Their home is a three-storied building surrounded by high walls. The portico is straight ahead from the gate. To the left lies a tiny garden, a gravel path running around it. Tall iron lamp-posts. Rantideb's driver escorts me to the house. A few shallow steps lead up to an enormous veranda, on the right-hand side of which is a mahogany door at least eight feet high, studded with brass motifs. Next to the door is a red granite statue of Ganesha and a pigeon-holed wooden partition-frame from Rajasthan. A yellow leafy Chinese bamboo plant peeps out from behind the partition, swooping down on the statue of Ganesha. The house obviously belongs to a person of good taste.

As soon as the driver rings the bell, a man in a white service uniform opens the huge door and steps aside. 'Please come in,' he says.

I step inside and am stunned by the opulence. The floor downstairs is wooden, polished, shining. The hall is no less than 1500 square feet in area, ending in a veranda with French windows that are folded at present, bringing into view a slice of garden that looks miraculously green. The high walls at the end of the garden signal the periphery of the property. There are a few trees in the garden, I can clearly see a mango tree and a chikoo tree. The sky has almost darkened this side – this is the east, then.

The young man in white uniform can't be eighteen yet. He asks me to sit down. I select a slim sofa rather than one of the leather-covered settees you sink into. Since I am here for a job, it wouldn't be right for me to settle down comfortably. Sakshi and Hitabrata had me admitted to Modern High School – etiquette and courtesy are as indispensable to me as breathing, I would never make a mistake with such things. Even after being locked into a room for three days without food, I did not wolf down my first meal noisily.

I sit down. And remain seated. All I can see is the silent movement of white uniforms. Now and then phones at both ends of the hall ring softly. A Chinese girl arrives a little later, a wicker basket in her hand. Throwing a glance at me, she goes upstairs.

I had expected a barrage of questions as soon as I arrived. I would have to keep telling small interlinked stories. I was bound to be asked to produce my tax-payer card and passport. The problems of a current address as well as a permanent one would shake my world once again. If writing a novel about a woman with no name or family appears to be so difficult, people are bound to be confused if there is no verifiable evidence of a flesh-and-blood birth, family, education, home, and conscious and subconscious lives. And I will have to cover all these gaps with stories. I have come prepared, but my preparations remain imprisoned at the tip of my tongue while I observe the architecture of Radheshyam House.

The area to the left of the big door seems to be Budhaditya's chamber – the portion with steel chairs and small couches is probably a waiting room for clients. The walls of the next hall are lined from floor to ceiling with law books. Two flights of stairs wind upwards and downwards from the left, up to the first floor and down to the sunken dining hall. To the east of the dining hall is another row of French windows and, beyond those, the garden.

Paintings have been arranged with great attention on the three landings upstairs. Most of the contemporary Indian painters are present here: Jatin Das, Ramkumar and Manjit Bawa are easily recognizable, the rest aren't unknown but because I have not registered their style in the past, I cannot recollect their names – oh, yes, I have just recognised Arpita Caur again… This tendency towards ascent and descent is very interesting. And because of this, the environment here has given rise to a complexity dependent on multiple senses. It's possible that intricate and delicate choices are the hallmark of this house; they certainly fill the thoughts of those who are waiting, with plenty of time at their disposal.

I have told Sukul that I will be back in an hour and a half. Ninety minutes have passed already. Is anyone even at home? In my mind's eye I can see what is going on up on the roof of Dinratri. Sukul is sitting with an expressionless face, it is getting dark, Roo is in bed, silent. My experience tells me Sukul is nice to Roo in my presence. Sukul talks to Roo in my presence – but when I'm not there, he's blind, he's deaf when it comes to Roo. The more helpless I am proving to be, the more Sukul's breath is closing in on me. Yesterday he brought me a rose, a red rose. The pulse in his forehead hammers a different kind of ambition these days. He has no one to call his own. I'll be in danger if he decides to cling to me, real danger. I hear footsteps on the stairs. The Chinese girl comes downstairs and leaves. Ishwari had to wait a little longer. Anyone who knew the emptiness, the stillness of waiting this way also knew it made every nerve gradually lose confidence.

Eventually a freshly bathed woman in a white salwar kameez, touching sixty, came downstairs. The Chinese girl must have been here for some kind of beauty treatment for this very woman. Tall, beautiful, in a state of eternal health, she looked at Ishwari in surprise. 'You are…?' she asked.

Ishwari had risen to her feet. Joining her palms in greeting, she said, 'I'm Ishwari.'

'Yes…?' she said. She hadn't understood.

'Mr Rantideb Mullick sent me.'

Finally things fell into place. 'Oh, yes of course… Really, Kalicharan!' she called out loudly. The white uniform who had opened the door was Kalicharan. 'Why didn't you take her to Bubu?' she asked.

'Dada asked her to wait.'

'How long ago?'

Kalicharan glanced at his watch. 'An hour and a half.'

'Honestly! You people are such idiots, I don't know what to say.' She took Ishwari's hand. 'Come with me.'

Upstairs, the woman knocked on the door on the right, once, twice. When there was no response, she said, 'Bubu? Bubu?' but still there wasn't any reply. 'What's the matter?' she asked Ishwari of all people, and turned the knob to open the door and peep in. Looking over her shoulder, Ishwari saw a handsome young man of about thirty-five asleep on the sofa, a thick paintbrush dangling from his fingers. A crutch leaned against the wall next to the sofa.

'Are you feeling all right, Bubu?' As soon as the lady touched him, Bibaswan sat up. His eyes turned to Ishwari. Drawing his crutch to himself, he stood up, he could not have been happy about appearing before a stranger in such a mentally unprepared state. Bibaswan looked at her with a frown. His mother said, 'Rantideb has sent Ishwari. Have you any idea how long you've kept her waiting? More than an hour and a half.'

Bibaswan's expression did not change, he said, 'Excuse me,' and limped away, possibly to the toilet.

'Sit down, Ishwari,' the lady said. 'Bubu will tell you everything himself. He needs a friend, some-one who can also help him with his daily life. Would you like coffee, or do you prefer tea? No, you must have a glass of water first. I'll send Kalicharan. The boy's such an idiot, he didn't even offer you a glass of water. He's new, you see. The governor of my house-hold is Umapati. He's on leave. Oh, and my name is Sita.' Instructing Ishwari to see her before leaving, she withdrew.

Bibaswan seemed more collected when he emerged from the toilet. She was about to rise to her feet when

he said, 'That's all right.' A trace of annoyance mingled with the absent-mindedness in his voice. His
brow was still creased, but he no longer looked sleepy.
Ishwari tried to match the person before her with
Rantideb's description of Bibaswan.

Bibaswan fiddled with the long, tapered paintbrush lying on the glass table and suddenly said, as
though offering justification, 'They suggested this.
My family.'

'Suggested what?' asked Ishwari.

'Hiring a friend. Several people came but... I
don't think this will work.'

Ishwari felt a lump grow in her throat. She had
been sitting downstairs all by herself for such a long
time, her Roo was languishing with a reluctant companion. Gourohori didn't know she had run out of
rice, neither she nor Roo had eaten anything today.
She had no money now – for the first time she had
decided to ask Sukul for some money, she would tell
him to put the cash on the table, she would never be
able to take it directly from his hands. She was afraid.
If she were close enough to him, his breath would
touch her skin.

'You're right,' she said, 'friendship can't be hired.'

'You agree with me?' Bibaswan was surprised.

'Yes.'

Kalicharan came in with two cups of coffee and two glasses of water, and put them down and left.

'Then why did you agree to this assignment?'

She took her time to answer. 'Work is love made visible. If I perform it with love, any task can be successful. Friendship can be nurtured – if a kindred soul is compassionate, friendship can be a deliberate outcome. Whether someone is in fact a kindred soul can only be judged after two individuals get to know one another. Whether someone is compassionate or not can be judged by opening up one's heart a little to them. Even if friendship cannot be hired, a compassionate kindred soul certainly can. And friendship may develop in a month or two or three. Besides, I believe friendly behaviour is the first condition of friendship.'

'But once the friendship develops, will the monetary transactions not influence the relationship?' Bibaswan enquired.

Her stomach felt queasy, there was no point in jabbering away. She looked at Bibaswan. He continued, 'Friendship is between equals, isn't it?'

'I don't know for sure. I have never had a friend.'

'How ironic. Someone who has never had a friend is being given an assignment to be a friend. I pity you.'

Iswari's head reeled. She said, 'May I leave now?'

'Yes, of course.' Bibaswan rose to his feet. So did she. And the moment she did, everything went dark. Blindly she took one step, then another. The ground shook beneath her feet, she told herself, 'No, I have to walk, I have to walk up to the Lake, I have to walk all the way to the end of the novel – it'll mean suffering, but I must walk.'

She took the thirty steps from the sofa to the door, and then slipped on masses of clouds, sinking to the floor.

—

Four or five seconds passed. She regained consciousness even as she was falling. As Bibaswan approached her on his crutch, she tried to stand up. It was such a large room, Bibaswan would take some time to reach her – Ishwari hauled herself up in the meantime using the doorknob as leverage.

'How did this happen? Are you all right?' Bibaswan asked, surprised and troubled.

'Just… my head… I'm fine.' Ishwari was extremely embarrassed. She was still teetering somewhere within herself.

'Does this often happen to you?'

She looked at Bibaswan sharply. This young man had kept her waiting for an hour and a half without reason – or was he so feeble as to fall asleep every now and then?

'No, never,' she answered.

'If you hadn't got up yourself I wouldn't have been able to help you, I'd have to call Sukhendu or one of the other servants.'

'I'm all right.'

'You'd better take a few minutes' rest, don't you think? See how you feel.'

'No, I'm fine. I'll go now.'

'Are you sure?'

'Yes.'

'All right, I'll tell them, they'll drop you home in the car.' How could Ishwari refuse? She had no money.

Bibaswan held the door open for Ishwari. 'I'm going to Vizag tomorrow morning. I'll be back the same night, so you can start the day after tomorrow.'

She felt as though the clock on the wall had stopped ticking, and time was preparing to run backwards – a job, some work – maybe the post was nothing but a combination of nurse, housekeeper and personal attendant, but the money was significant to her. And someone like Bibaswan could not possibly spend all his time among servants, he could not tolerate the company of some ayah from the slums or some coarse, unsophisticated nurse. He needed someone to talk to and Ishwari had the ability to provide what Bibaswan wanted from a hired friend.

Overcoming her numbness, Ishwari asked, 'What time should I come?'

'Is eleven all right with you?'

'Absolutely.'

'See you then.' The door closed.

On her way downstairs, Ishwari halted for a moment. She had not seen this particular drawing from the hall. An ink sketch. This was Rameshwar Broota's 'Champion'! She had seen it at the biennale exhibition at the Triveni Kala Sangam. The subject of the drawing was a perspiring athlete, all his muscles sharply etched, confidence – tremendous self-confidence – radiating from his jaws; only his eyes held a dangerous hollowness, a complete blankness. Round, bulging eyes that had never blinked. It was the kind of art that captivated. She had experienced it then, and she was experiencing it now. How strange the eyes were, how could the people here bear to live with this sketch?

Suddenly someone behind her addressed her as 'Madam'. Turning around, she saw a man in a white uniform, there were probably no women employees here. 'Madam left this for you. She had to go out.' He held out an envelope; she took it and knew at first touch that it contained money. How strange, how did Sita know that Bibaswan would approve of her as a hired friend?

—

Getting out of the car, Ishwari rushed up to the terrace, eager to take Roo in her arms. Seeing her run in, Montu and Prabir poked their heads out of the office. She barely managed to avoid colliding with a boarder who was coming down the stairs with his luggage. When she stepped onto the roof, she stopped, overwhelmed. Sukul was pacing the roof restlessly with Roo in his arms. Roo's head was resting on his shoulder. His eyes were shut.

Tears pricked at Ishwari's eyelids. Have I misunderstood Sukul's intentions? Do I dislike him simply because he is not well-educated and drives a taxi? If Sukul had taken care of Roo like this for three hours – or had it been longer? – Ishwari was grateful to him. Sukul, we have no relationship with you, yet you are doing so much for us. Your generosity makes me feel small. There's no one like you, Sukul, in the life that I am familiar with. Everyone is selfish – they care for nothing but their own needs, they cheat one another, they use people and cast them aside. Their eyes are

like those of Rameshwar Broota's 'Champion', so
blank they do not blink – what if blinking means losing an opportunity, the opportunity to become the
champion, the opportunity to remain the champion?

I have no words to express my gratitude, Sukul.

Sukul spotted her. 'Oh, you're back,' his voice was
anxious. 'Roo has been throwing up.'

'Again? Why? Did you see him eat anything in
particular?'

'He ate some biscuits when I wasn't looking.'

'Biscuits? Where did he get biscuits?'

Sukul lowered his eyes. 'I'd got them for myself.'

Ishwari reached for Roo, took him into the room
and set him down on the bed. 'Roo,' she called out.

Roo didn't open his eyes.

'Roo,' she called again, 'Roo! Roo! Roo!' Forcing
his eyelids up, Ishwari found his eyeballs still. 'What's
happened to him?' she screamed. She wanted to
bite this pup of death into wakefulness. And at that
moment, Roo poured himself out in a torrent of yel-
lowish water, bringing her immense relief.

—

At about eight in the evening, Roo's stomach ache
reached intolerable proportions. He contorted his little limbs in agony. Sukul hadn't come in his taxi today

– he had returned the vehicle to its owner after work. He picked Roo up in his arms, Ishwari wrapped him in whatever sheets and towels she had, and clutching a bottle of glucose water and three thousand rupees in an envelope, she found a taxi. Dr Chitrabhanu Ghosh's prescription said he saw patients at home on Sunday evening. There was no time to phone ahead. With only a grain of hope, Ishwari rushed to his residence in Park Circus.

They tumbled into a chamber full of waiting patients. At the sight of Roo's drooping head, ashen face and laboured breathing, no one protested, no one stopped her. She barged in like a mad woman, saying, 'Dr Ghosh, the boy's unconscious. Terrible vomiting, terrible stomach ache.' Someone took Roo from her arms.

Dr Ghosh took one look at him and said, 'He needs an injection to relieve the pain. At once.'

That was as far as Ishwari heard, she tried to say, I have the money, I have the money for treatment, and then, for the second time today, her head spun and she lost consciousness.

Eventually, Roo's breathing returned to normal and they went home. At about ten o'clock the boy slipped into a deep sleep. Gourohori had got out of bed despite his own high fever to sit with Roo. When

Roo fell asleep, he said, 'Why must God torture a mere child this way? When he came he used to talk, he used to chatter, he'd ask for stories. And now he's completely silent.' Eyes bright, he left the room.

Sukul was leaning against the wall near the door. He told Ishwari, 'I've left some food for you on the table, don't forget to eat.'

Was he leaving? She would be terribly alone if he forsook her now. She looked at him defiantly and said, 'No, you're not leaving tonight, Sukul, you'll stay the night. How could you even think of abandoning us in this hour of danger? What if there's another crisis?'

Sukul ran his eyes over her unhesitatingly. 'I wouldn't have left, I would be close by, on the verandah at Maharani guest house.'

'No, you must stay here, sleep on the roof. I'm afraid, lonely. All this time I've lived alone with my fears – fears like thousands of miles of black earth – but tonight I want to be afraid with you here. If Roo suffers again I want to tell you, "Do something, save him." And if Roo sleeps all night I want to call you in the morning and say, "Look, Sukul, how peacefully Roo is sleeping. No pain, no tears. Maybe he's recovered." I want to share all this with you, Sukul. Let Roo sleep, let's eat together, you and I.'

They ate together.

Then Sukul took a sheet and went out on the roof to sleep. Ishwari sat down by her child and said, 'There were so many dangers in your mother's womb too, weren't there, Roo? For each baby who chokes to death when its umbilical cord is wrapped around its throat, its mother's womb is its tomb. And what about the foetuses who cannot survive more than three months in the darkness of gestation? Or those who are affected by their mothers' diseases? Or the ones struck by jaundice? It is their mothers who dispense death, who create death. I have saved you from all those deaths, you have overcome so many dangers, can't you do it again this time?'

When the mother's womb kills the child, does anyone hold the mother responsible? Is she called a murderer or hauled off to jail? Only mothers can dispense the kind of death neither nature nor civilization can question.

'Get well, Roo, I promise you'll go to school. Look, here's the money – I'll take you for an ultrasound first thing in the morning. The hospital is nearby, I'll carry you.'

Sometimes I think being alive is nothing but watching my own life as much as it can be watched. Don't worry, Roo, whether there's anyone else or not, I am here with you. The pages of my novel have burnt to ashes. I am looking at you, at your future, with the eyes that saw it burn. I am looking at your life along with mine, as a whole.

'Roo, this bond of birth is wonderful, I will gaze at your face all night. I will wipe away the slightest pain with love – with magic, Roo, magic, magic!' As she spoke, Ishwari fell asleep. Some time later she opened her eyes to see Sukul standing near her feet. Sitting up, she asked, 'What is it, Sukul?' She covered her breasts swiftly.

'It's morning,' said Sukul.

'Morning? But it's dark outside.'

'No, it's four o'clock, the birds are awake. I have to go, I have to get the taxi to the stand.'

I stand up and put my hand on his shoulder. 'You've done so much for us, Sukul, you've done whatever I asked, and I've developed a sort of right over you in these past two months. I feel as though you belong to us. To me and Roo.' Sukul lowers my hand from his shoulder slowly, his face is barely visible.

He says, 'I feel the same way about you and Roo. I don't have anyone to call my own, either.'

'Really, Sukul? Let it stay that way, let there be nobody but us whom you can call your own, Sukul.' Raising my head, I smell the sharp tang of tobacco on his body. I recognised the same smell on Roo yesterday – Sukul had been carrying him in his arms. Waves of gratitude surge in my heart, which does not realise it is dawn. They rise, they advance. They retreat, they advance again. With the same hand that Sukul lowered lightly, I clutch his shirt, my mind still foggy with sleep. I feel a strong urge to be kissed, to accept any foolish caress that is offered. My body merges with the animal desire for sex. For a moment, I am reminded of the scene where Bibaswan was asleep – of 'him', his shapely, bare body when 'he' stands on the balcony smoking. I remember that I have received nothing but degradation in life. I bury my face in Sukul's chest, press myself against his stiff body which has turned to stone, push him up against the wall, and meet his thick, soft lips.

Instantly Sukul wraps his arms around me with the force of an uncoiled spring. A hot mouth covers my breasts. I push Sukul's head down to my stomach – he cannot control himself, he cannot deal with foreplay. Grabbing my waist, he makes me lie down on the floor. He takes off our clothes himself, and plunges in like an amateur. I let the inexperienced boy into my impatient, liquid darkness, tumbling like an injured bee, humming, and somewhere in the distance two freight trains ram into each other and are fused together. I accumulate the wounds deep inside me, in nooks and crannies, fearful of their ending, and I begin to count the acts of oppression because within my arid self every single one cries out like a sexual act. I scatter the sounds of this tyranny all over my empty room. And at this moment Roo sits up in bed.

With a muffled scream, Ishwari tried to push Sukul off her. 'Roo?' she said, making an attempt to get up.

'Ma?' answered Roo.

'Sukul!' screamed Ishwari.

Roo climbed off the bed, saying, 'No!' Ishwari grabbed a fistful of Sukul's hair and tried to push him off but Sukul's limbs clamped down on her like a vice. I scold Roo. 'Go back to bed, Roo. For god's sake, go.'

Roo retreated a step, then another. Ishwari wept piteously. Sukul continues to have sex with all his power, I continue to have sex with all my tolerance, Ishwari groaned, and amid this wrestling, Roo stood by in the first light of day like a wondering angel. A little later, a most barbaric explosion of sound accompanying the inconsiderate ejaculation of semen echoed through the room.

—

Ishwari knocked and entered the room and saw Biba-swan sitting in a deckchair on the balcony holding a glass of lassi, facing the trees in the garden. For the first time, she noticed how lovely the room was. The floor was of white marble flecked with brown, the walls were peanut-coloured. The bed was to the left of the door. The room rose one level to an area with a revolving chair and a huge desk with a dark green cut-glass table lamp, a computer and some decorative objects. Opposite the bed was a beautiful seating arrangement. At the back, glass racks stacked with books rose to the ceiling. To the right of the bed, on the other side of the door, a pair of oak wardrobes ran down the length of the wall, a panel of mirrors stretched across their doors. Three large paintings hung on the walls above the bed, near the balcony and behind the sofa. Everything from the bedspread to the upholstery was coloured brown. Different shades of brown, both light and dark. And to Ishwari, brown was the finest colour, because brown was the colour of the intellect. Brown was the colour of the journey from primitive to civilised.

Beyond the workspace was the half-moon balcony suspended over the little garden. And to declare their love for this balcony, the branches of the mango tree laden with tender blooms had bent down to embrace it. The room was so large that even with designated areas for sleeping, sitting and working, there was plenty of space left over. She felt that it was to cater to Bibaswan's convenience that the room had been turned into a combination of study, music room and artist's studio.

It was a music room since a music system and other pieces of sound equipment were placed on a waist-high chest of drawers in the south-east corner. Next to it stood an acoustic guitar. A tanpura in a leather jacket, an ektara on top of the chest of drawers, numerous CDs and DVDs, a plasma TV on the wall. An artist's studio, because in the centre of the sprawling room was an easel with a large canvas mounted on it, a thick base of brown had been painted on it and left to dry. Both the upper and lower racks of a low, wide teapoy were strewn with tubes of paint; brushes peeped out of a large basket on the floor. The room was essentially neat but there were books, CDs, paint and other things scattered everywhere. On the bed lay a copy of Tony Morrison's *Beloved*, a bookmark sticking out of it. A book Ishwari had neither read nor touched.

Bibaswan looked distracted when she walked up to the balcony. 'I was wondering whether to phone and tell you not to come,' he said.

Ishwari's heart jumped into her mouth in fear of losing her job. 'Oh,' she said, 'but I don't have a phone.'

'Really? No phone? How strange. Everyone has one these days.'

'Should I leave?'

A bird flew up to the mango tree and perched on a branch. It was yellow and reddish brown, with a tiny beak. Without replying, Bibaswan watched the bird with narrowed eyes, saying, 'Incredible, this looks like the same bird as yesterday. It's a fantastic bird. Can you find my glasses, please?'

Ishwari couldn't find the glasses anywhere, she returned to say. Bibaswan stirred impatiently. 'In the toilet then. Quick. It'll fly away.'

Despite her reluctance, she entered the toilet. Spotting the gold–framed glasses on the marble counter, she took them to Bibaswan. Placing his empty glass on the table, Bibaswan put on the spectacles and began to observe the bird with keen attention. She stood by, wondering what she should be doing. She wasn't sure exactly what she had been hired to do. Remembering that she had already spent most of the three thousand rupees, she picked up the empty glass and wandered off. But Bibaswan called her back. 'You're not interested in birds, are you?'

Why this question? she wanted to ask. Just because I didn't get excited at the sight of a tiny sunbird, does it mean I'm indifferent to birds? There are several stages that precede birdwatching. It needs mental preparation, enormous concentration. How can I watch birds until I know whether I'm staying or going? Instead, she said, 'Oh no, I love birds. This one's a sunbird.'

Bibaswan looked at her for the first time. 'Sunbird? Can you identify this bird?'

'Yes, it's very rare. It's native to Bengal…'

'There are some books on birds in the third row of that bookshelf there. Can you bring me *Bengal Birds* from that bunch? Let's see what it has to say.'

Ishwari fetched the book. Bibaswan leafed through it, scanned the photograph of the sunbird, and said, 'Sit down, Ishwari.' When she did, he told her, 'Ishwari is a lovely name but every time I have to use it I am reminded that I am a mere human. How do we solve this problem?'

'You can call me Isha. That's my name too.'

'What does it mean?'

'There's no precise meaning. Ish has a meaning but not Isha, Ish is the same as Ishwar, meaning 'god'. And Ee… sha means plough.'

'Very well then. Ee… sha it is.'

'Fine.'

'May I be informal with you?'

'Of course.'

'Mumbai. Rantideb Uncle said you hate Mumbai. Why do you hate Mumbai?' Bibaswan's cold eyes grazed her eyes, her cheeks, the tip of her nose.

The question reminded Ishwari of Roo. He was locked in the room now, with only a rubber sheet, some water and food. There was no one with him. 'When will you be back, Ma?' Roo had asked. What could she have said in response? She didn't know herself. When she returned, maybe she would discover that they had broken down the door and taken Roo away by force. She was surprised they hadn't made a single enquiry about Roo even after all this time. Or had they made their enquiries without her knowledge? Perhaps, just like they didn't want her, they didn't want Roo either. 'No one wants us, Roo, no one wants us,' she said to herself.

Bibaswan probably realised she didn't want to talk about Mumbai, so he changed the subject and asked her, 'What's the reason for this saffron sari? Do you wear this sari all the time?'

She lowered her eyes and smiled. She didn't say this was her only sari, she didn't say she had got rid of all her possessions some time ago to lighten her burden. It had been foolish of her. A foolishness she repented every day now. And since 'regret comforts one', she had been mulling over all the foolish acts she had performed in her life – all day, all night, in her sleep, in her nightmares. All the foolish things she had done pursued the dangerous present she lived in.

'A matter of faith?' asked Bibaswan. 'Or is there another reason?'

She smiled again.

'Won't you tell me, Isha?' Bibaswan used the informal *tumi*. The young man's brow was no longer furrowed, his gaze was soft. Ishwari looked at him fully. Ishwari was incapable of providing the effervescent company Bibaswan needed during his convalescence. She was withdrawn, bore qualities that had to be discovered with effort. So Bibaswan would have a pleasant time with Ishwari before throwing his crutch away. Ishwari's journey from one level to another would keep him sufficiently occupied, and the objective for which Rantideb or this family had appointed Ishwari would be successfully realised. Even Bibaswan had begun to understand this – the more interest he felt in Ishwari, the more successful her appointment would prove. And as everyone knew, this interest was the most significant aspect of any relationship that involved giving and taking.

'It's not exactly a matter of faith,' answered Ishwari. 'I am an atheist, I cannot relate in the least to the connections between this colour and the Hindu religion. But I sense that this colour bestows some sort of purity on my soul, my fear disappears, I feel honest – as though there's a way through all the complexities of life.'

Bibaswan was deep in thought, biting his lips. 'May I have some water?' he asked.

Ishwari rose and fetched a glass of water from the bedside table. In the last half hour she had understood her role at Radheshyam House. Draining his glass, Bibaswan rose to his feet, leaning on his crutch. 'Can I help?' she asked.

'No, I'll tell you if I need you to. Ring the bell for Sukhendu, Isha, let him bring you a cup of coffee.'

'Yes, I will, would you like some?'

'No, I haven't had a bath yet. I'll have some after lunch.'

'Do you want a bath? Should I call someone?'

'Later. Let me show you something first.' Ishwari followed Bibaswan to the canvas. 'Tania, my late wife,' declared Bibaswan. Ishwari now noticed some scratches on the canvas that suggested the face of a woman. 'Something strange is happening in my life,' Bibaswan continued. 'I am trying to paint my wife, my wife Tania whom I have known for so long, but I can't.' Bibaswan looked at the canvas combatively. 'Why is this happening? I'm trying to paint Tania the way I see her in my mind, but it isn't working. Strange frames pop up in my head, some very strange moments. Tania still poses for me all the time, extraordinary poses: there's the Tania in Delhi, restless in the heat, running towards me from a distance, I can see the image shimmering in hot air; in Vizag and in Pune it's a different Tania; and in Mumbai, with friends, at parties, drinking beer – so many different Tanias appear before my eyes... We travelled so much, Isha! I remember it all so well. You wouldn't believe how pretty she was, apple-cheeked, tall – but when I try to paint her I can't capture anything. Strange, isn't it.'

Ishwari looked at Bibaswan in surprise.

'Can you tell my why? And yet, believe me, I'm a good painter. This one's mine, after all.' Bibaswan pointed to the painting hanging over the bed. Four by three, oil on canvas. A reclining nude against a dusty backdrop, coils of hair suspended in the darkness, both arms stretched out over her head, a lotus bud in one hand, a small pot with a flame rising out of it in the other. Very pale hues, even the orange and yellow of the flames were subdued. The painting was titled 'Just Finished'.

'This is yours?' Ishwari exclaimed. 'It's fantastic!'

Bibaswan looked hurt. 'This is Tania too,' he said.

'I treated her as a goddess, as Ishwari. I drew hundreds of nudes of her, you know. I made her sit in front of me, stared for hours at every pore on her skin, and now I can't even make a pencil sketch without the help of a photograph? I feel like such a failure. I thought I was her real lover, the finest among all her lovers, but I was wrong.' Bibaswan hobbled away, and Ishwari noticed that he could not put his weight on his left foot.

Bibaswan opened one of the wardrobe doors. Canvases of different sizes lay inside, and Ishwari realised what Bibaswan was trying to show her. She pulled out the topmost canvas. Bibaswan pointed at it and said, 'Look, look at this. Is this her? No. Is this Tania? No, not at all.' Bibaswan shrugged. 'How funny.' He went back to his bed, discarded his crutch and lay down. Ishwari had no idea what she should do next. She tried to act naturally, and said, 'Your bath must be ready, let me check.'

—

She ran into Sita as she came out of the room. With a smile, Sita said, 'Ah, you're here? I didn't even know.' Sita was dressed in gym clothes, she was glowing with health. 'What's Bubu doing?' she asked.

'He's resting.'

Clucking regretfully, Sita said, 'He can't take it – I can see that clearly. Perhaps he should have spent some more time in Maryland.'

They went downstairs together, and entered the dining hall. Sita turned to her and said urgently, 'There's a room just above this one, Ishwari. You can use it. There's a wardrobe in there, a bed too. I know Bubu, there's no knowing when his mood will sour, and he won't allow anyone into his room. He's been moody since childhood. He was ten years old when I came into this family. He's always been incredibly quiet, cold, he didn't want to talk to anyone. But he liked me. I'm probably the only one in this family who's close to him today. Please don't keep standing, do sit down.'

She pulled up a chair. It appeared Sita was Biba-swan's stepmother. 'Coffee?' asked Sita.

Ishwari nodded.

'Umapati,' Sita called.

'So your Umapati is back?'

'Oh, it's a big relief, Ishwari! Do you know we don't get our meals in this house when Umapati isn't here? I keep saying Umapati is my *upapati* – my second husband.' She winked. 'It's just as well he doesn't understand what I mean.'

A middle-aged man in white uniform came up to

the table. He wore thick glasses and a distant expression. It hadn't been obvious in the hall, but the part of the house directly below Budhaditya Bagchi's chamber was an open kitchen. It was an eye-catching, colourful space with yellow and snuff-coloured tiles. Sita told Umapati very sweetly, 'Make us a couple of small dosas, Umapati. Have you made the mint chutney?'

'Yes, Madam,' answered Umapati. 'Anything else?'

'Coffee. Listen, this madam is Bubu's friend, she will come every day from now on, look after her, all right? Make nice things for her to eat. Serve her lunch in Bubu's room, or else he will have to eat by himself, and Bubu gets angry when he has to eat by himself.'

Umapati joined his palms respectfully towards Ishwari.

'Why did Bubu send his omelette back this morning?' Sita asked.

'His wish,' Umapati declared. 'One moment he wants an omelette, the next moment he sends the omelette back.'

Sita smiled. 'All right, go now, I'm starving after the gym. Remember, Ishwari, Umapati is an institution, he goes back to the time before Bubu was born – he might even scold you now and then.' Sita poured Ishwari a glass of water from the jug. 'Call Sukhendu whenever you need help. Bubu likes him.' She yawned delicately. 'Rantideb had asked me to give you an advance of three thousand rupees. Did you get it?'

'Yes.'

'Listen, I may not be home all the time, but an envelope with your payment will be kept in the drawer of Bubu's bedside table every day. Manoj takes care of all that. A thousand different payments for a thousand different people, he'll make arrangements for yours too. It's best to make daily payments. If he forgets for some reason, don't feel embarrassed to remind him.'

'When I arrived Bibaswan told me he had been thinking of phoning and asking me not to come,' Ishwari said.

'Really? Probably because Kasturi is supposed to be here.'

'Kasturi?' She was afraid, Kasturi must be a caregiver like her.

'Kasturi was originally Tania's friend. When Tania and Bibaswan went to Sydenham to study, so did Kasturi – she was Tania's roommate there. Then Bibaswan joined a prominent advertising agency in Mumbai, in the creative team. Tania and Kasturi joined another one. Tania was crazy about having a baby. And then of course… Kasturi loved Tania very much, she's very fond of Bibaswan too. She visits him sometimes. She went to America with us and has also visited Bubu after he returned. She was planning to come today as well, but probably won't make it. She's a busy girl.'

Umapati had got the food ready, he placed crisp golden-white dosas on the table and arranged three different vegetables around them in small bowls, some sambar and chutneys of various kinds.

'Dessert?' said Sita. 'Umapati, give me one of those laddoos the Chauhans sent. Will you have some dates from Al Basra, Ishwari? I won't have lunch later, Umapati.'

Ishwari felt no embarrassment as all the food – lime juice, pears, fried fish – appeared before her. Her eyes smarted, thin trickles of blood filled the veins and arteries in her eyes as she remembered she had left some mashed rice and potato for Roo in a bowl. Maybe Roo was picking at it with a spoon. Maybe ants were swarming over the food. As the hours went by the rice would release water. Roo hated that, he would use his spoon to remove the water before eating his rice. That was Roo's only game in his locked room.

—

This is what happens; this novel holds me responsible repeatedly. This novel considers Ishwari, her wants and all that she has been denied since childhood to be extraordinary; it depicts her as an uncomplicated and persecuted orphan. It is biased in her favour. I want to step aside from this novel, or else I will be led astray by the irrelevance of unfavourable fortunes. Should I knowingly participate in a novel that wants to play snakes and ladders with me? I want to let go of Ishwari – let her remain in there alone. But it is Ishwari who holds on to me – I kick her, she retreats. In Radheshyam House, Sita and I continue eating.

When we have finished and are sipping our coffee, Sukhendu appears in the dining hall, saying, 'Dada is asking for you, Madam.' It is me that Sukhendu says this to. I push back my chair and jump up. I feel nervous. Bibaswan needs me? The burden of this need seems disproportionate to my pay packet.

Sita says, 'Finish your meal.'

I look at her gratefully and say, 'May I find out what he wants first?'

'All right then,' she says with a smile. Sometimes, women do like women. I like Sita very much. I feel I haven't had a woman in my life for so long. I feel this emptiness strongly enough that it makes my heart stop suddenly. What does a woman have if she has no woman in her life? Women are very important in women's lives. A man makes a woman realise she's a woman; a woman makes her realise she's human.

Back upstairs, Bibaswan is restless. He seems lonely, and when he's lonely he's melancholy. 'Where were you, Isha?'

I am embarrassed. Avoiding any reference to the fact that I was eating, I say, 'I was with Sita Aunty.'

'Come here. Don't go away without telling me.'

My insides tremble. I feel as though Bibaswan is going to hold the end of my saffron sari in his balled-up fist and look for someone in there. Is it right to ask for someone this way? In my head I want to know, and I walk towards him step by step. Bibaswan averts his eyes, my back tingles, my breasts ache with pain. I know the reason for all this. No one has called me in this way in such a long time; even this novel understands my agony. Bibaswan sucks up my rawness. When I go up to him, he says, 'Choose what you like from the CDs there and put it on.' He rests his face in his hand, his thoughts gather between his eyebrows. I select one of the seven or eight CDs scattered on the bed. With his eyes, Bibaswan instructs me how to operate his music system. A red light blinks twice when the song is about to start, I feel that I will burst like a bubble and disappear from Bibaswan's room the instant it begins to play. I am tearful at the prospect. Then the music plays, taking these moments out of the ceremony of my life to a climax…

Log kehte hain ajnabi tum ho
Ajnabi meri zindagi tum ho
Log kehte hain ajnabi tum ho

People say you're a stranger
Stranger, you're my life
People say you're a stranger

I look at Bibaswan in trepidation and see that it is me he is looking at. His eyes tell me I have done well. I have proved myself worthy of spending the next four or five months with him. Then he looks away, submerging himself somewhere unknown.

Mujhko apna shareek-e-gham kar lo
Yun akele bahut dukhi tum ho
Ajnabi meri zindagi tum ho

Help me feel your sorrows too
You, who have seen so much alone
Stranger, you are my life

Very slowly, our emptiness disappears. The long couplets of surrender travel from me to him. I stand leaning against the chest of drawers. I want to ask Sukhendu for another cup of coffee. The coffee here has a wonderful flavour. Sita said the coffee beans have arrived recently from Brazil.

—

It was seven by the time Ishwari returned to Lansdowne Road. She had been fretting since five, but had been unable to ask Bibaswan when she could leave. Bibaswan spent the entire afternoon on the sofa with his eyes closed. He didn't say a word, didn't have lunch — she felt afraid of his grim expression and bloodshot eyes. Once, just once, she tried to leave Bibaswan's presence, and he said immediately, 'Where are you going, Ishwari?'

Bibaswan had addressed her as Ishwari of his own accord. Why? 'I thought you wanted to be alone, so I was going into the other room. That's the room Sita Aunty has asked me to use if I need to.'

Tossing the remote control for the CD player on the sofa, Bibaswan said, 'No, I don't want to be alone. I don't want to be alone for another minute. I do want to feel my grief but not alone. I want to expose my sorrow, my agony, my hopelessness to others.

Whenever I'm on the verge of a breakdown, Ishwari, my family moves away, they think I will not be able to restrain myself in their presence. They're wrong, they don't understand me. They understand themselves, but not me. Nobody in this house understands me. That is why I need you, Ishwari.'

Her soul was hurting again, her insides burned as though acid had been spilled all over them. She said, 'Someone who was struck by lightning cannot understand what a drowning person experiences, Bibaswan. The physical sensations are different, the battle for survival against each is different even if the fear of death is identical. Although I will be paid for these moments that I spend with you, even so, you know the mind has its deep hidden recesses. There's a recess like that in my mind too, Bibaswan, which refuses to remember who I am. You must try to forget yourself too. Let us see how much we can share with each other.'

'I have become very vulnerable,' answered Bibaswan. 'I should have been the one telling you what you just told me. I should be the one to say, "Ishwari, you are so nice, so sensitive... we can be friends, at least we can talk. Talking, talking, talking – such a vital urge, talking and listening. In the course of our conversation we might even forget that you won't come till eleven in the morning and will leave soon after sunset.'

'We might forget that I mustn't forget the envelope in your bedside table drawer when I leave. We might forget that that envelope is crucial for me, that I have to take it before I go.'

Bibaswan did not react to this roundabout bit of information. He said, 'There was a woman named Shami, she read Bengali literature in college, I don't remember who sent her. She had no depth. She was so boring, she'd be looking around the entire time – is there anything worth seeing in my room? Instead of looking after me she looked at the furniture. I got so angry. For heaven's sake, concentrate on me!' Bibaswan smiled for the first time. 'I had thought, this is good, she's studied Bengali, she can help me understand what's new in poetry here...' Bibaswan paused. 'But you are different, different from anyone I know. In this sari you look surreal. As though you're here and yet you're not. Or maybe you know how to be here and not here at the same time.'

From the very first day, Ishwari had been unable to size him up. Bibaswan knew she was nothing but hired help, but he felt no hesitation in acknowledging her qualities. And those qualities were not particularly strong – only abstract ideas. 'Here, but not here.'

Sita and Bibaswan, Ishwari mused, had tongues sharpened by intelligence. To them depth was something they could touch. Expression of grief was a right. Right now, Bibaswan wanted to stay with his emotions. He had chosen to live like this for some time. He was not insecure enough to want to forget his grief.

Ishwari was capable of analysing things thus, but she couldn't identify her own attitude towards Bibaswan. She remembered the ruined canvas she had pulled out from the wardrobe: Bibaswan's thwarted attempt to paint not just Tania but also a baby's face at Tania's breast. Bibaswan's constant attempts to do so made her unhappy and yet not quite unhappy. Her state of mind was reflected in the roughness of the mid-afternoon sky; in the heat of the sun, the chromatic notes of a ghazal made a potent statement – both pure and variant forms of the madhyam note entered the music:

> *Khud ko padta hoon, chhod deta hoon*
> *Ek barak roz mod deta hoon*
> *Is kadar zakhm hai nigahon mein*
> *Roz ek aaina tod deta hoon…*
> *Khud ko padta hoon, chhod deta hoon*

I read myself, I give up,
I turn a page every day
My gaze is wounded...
I break a mirror every day
I read myself, I give up

—

Ishwari opened the door to find Roo asleep. The stench of urine and shit hung in the air. Roo was curled up on his side. His head had slipped off the pillow. Standing in the middle of the room, astonished, Ishwari wondered whether her day had really passed like this, with Roo locked in his room for eight hours. Her life demanded such cruelty of her now; it had moved on to torture her son.

Ishwari bent over to take a closer look at Roo. It occurred to her that Roo might choke on his vomit and die. Both his body and the room smelled of vomit.

She still had about two-thirds of the three thousand rupees Sita had given her. She had stocked up on basic food for several days, but had forgotten to buy phenyl. Roo would have to be taken for a sonograph first thing in the morning. Ever since Roo had started taking the three medicines prescribed by Dr Chitrabhanu Ghosh, he had begun to cry while urinating. 'It's burning, Ma,' he told her. Roo had become unbelievably weak. He couldn't even cry properly. He hadn't had any protein for a month.

There were no mosquitoes here, but there were a lot of ants, swarms of them in some parts of the room. She quickly got out of her sari and cleaned the rubber sheet smeared with shit. She cleared away the used dishes, cleaned the room, then washed her sari and blouse and hung them up to dry on the terrace. As she did this, she thought of waking Roo and cuddling him, but something had gone wrong, somewhere – whenever Ishwari looked at Roo her vision dimmed, it seemed to her that a ghostly spirit had taken root within the lifeless boy. There was a sly distance in his eyes. A suspicion. A remoteness in his baby face. The sobbing, distressed, tragic Roo was lost. How difficult it was for her to reach out to her frail son now – and she knew this stemmed from her contingent guilt, which prevented her from disintegrating. 'It may take time, but Roo will forget all this sooner or later,' Ishwari explained to herself as she made a fresh bowl of rice.

She didn't pull Roo to herself. She circled him, drew a sheet over him. She went close to him but did not touch him, and her ribs ached with love. She went out on the terrace. The more this distance with her son weighed down on her, the faster she paced up and down.

Finally Roo awoke and stood at the door. He couldn't stand for too long these days. Ishwari ran to take his hand. After using the toilet, Roo took a plate of sticky rice and boiled potato and gazed at his food. Ishwari said, 'Eat, Roo. Eat while it's hot.'

'A little salt, please,' said Roo.

'I've added some already.'

'A little more.'

She gave him some more, Roo took a spoonful and said, 'Needs more salt,' and she stirred in some more. Roo took another spoonful and asked for more salt. He kept asking for salt. Even after she put a whole lump of salt on his plate, he asked for more. Eventually Ishwari lost her temper. Jerking the plate out of his hand, she drew him to her breast, smothering him, and cried out, 'What do you want to eat? I will give you whatever you want, we'll see what happens.'

'No,' said Roo. 'I'll throw up.'

She rubbed her face on her son's chest, she knocked her forehead against his feet. She cried herself into a state but Roo refused to tell her what he wanted to eat. Ishwari said, 'Let god give your illness to me, Roo, so that you can get better.'

Roo looked at her. 'I don't want this to happen to

you,' he said quietly.

—

Gourohori was so ill he couldn't move about at all, all he could do was lie in bed. Ishwari brought him his medicine. After Roo's sonography and blood, urine and stool tests, Ishwari went up to Gourohori's door with Roo in her arms.

'What did the doctor say?' the old man asked.

'The radiologist didn't say anything, we'll get the reports in the evening.'

Roo looked a little livelier today, perhaps because he had gone out. Raising his head, he said, 'I have huge worms in my stomach, Ma.'

'What? Who told you that?'

'The person who gave me the injection.'

'The one who took your blood?'

'Hmm.'

Gourohori said, 'Then there's nothing to worry about. As soon as the doctor gives you a very bitter medicine, the worms will run away.'

Roo curled his lips, smiling. Ishwari thought, maybe that's all it is, just worms.

'The maid had brought a young woman with her, she said she'll come back when you're here,' Gourohori told Ishwari.

'Why didn't you make her wait?' Ishwari exclaimed. 'When will she be back? I have to leave soon.'

'They've got a thousand things to take care of! Do you think they'll wait just because I ask them to? Don't worry, I'll send her upstairs when she's back.'

The woman came by just as Ishwari was leaving. A thin, quiet girl of about sixteen or seventeen named Preeti. Her eyes were dazzling. She had a scar on her hand, outlined by white marks. 'What's wrong with your hand, Preeti?' Ishwari asked.

'An insect bite,' Preeti answered, looking at the floor.

'Have you put anything on it?'

'No.'

'You'll have to be here all day, remember.'

Preeti nodded.

'What time should I come?'

'Come at eight in the morning, bring some fresh fish on your way from Lake Market. Can you do that? Do you know how to calculate prices? You can leave at eight in the evening.'

'How much will you pay, Didi?' asked the maid who had brought Preeti.

'You tell me.'

'A sick child means more responsibility, she'll have to clean up vomit… A thousand, all right? And one meal.'

'Can't afford it. Make it less than that.'

'Can't do it for less. This is a rich people's neighbourhood. They pay two or three thousand without batting an eyelid. It's only because I know your situation.'

Ishwari agreed. 'I'll buy you a dress, Preeti. When you're here you must wash your hands and feet and put on the dress before you attend to the child. Wash it before you leave in the evening.'

'Should I start tomorrow?'

'Yes, tomorrow.'

After they left, she sat for a minute at the window, even though she was late already.

She looked at the house behind theirs. That door was shut. 'He' wasn't here now. The house was bustling with activity. The owners talked animatedly in English and the servants in Bengali. 'Ma's done with her puja, send her breakfast, Akshay. Are you ready, Sunanda? I'm waiting, my dear.'

Leaning her forehead against the iron bars, Ishwari gazed in that direction a while longer – after this, she wouldn't have to lock Roo into the room when she left. Maybe today was the last day of her suffering, maybe this evening she would get to know that there was nothing seriously wrong with Roo, nothing at all

– he was unhappy, that was all.

But nothing like that happened. This novel maintained its control over Ishwari's life. There was a torrential downpour soon after she left Radheshyam House, the roads were waterlogged in minutes, cars stranded on the road. Ishwari had to wait under a poinciana tree, soaked to the bone, her body and head covered with scraps of yellow leaves.

When she finally left, it was late. Instead of returning to Dinratri, she went directly to collect Roo's medical reports. Even though she didn't understand their contents clearly, she was disconsolate. She took a taxi straight to Dr Ghosh's nursing home. He pored over the reports, and phoned the radiologist at once. Ishwari trembled as Dr Ghosh apologised and then explained to her the silent spread of Roo's illness. Both his kidneys were full of tiny stones, like sand. Innumerable stones. Ishwari listened, the gritty taste of sand on her tongue, their particles gathering on her feet, her shoes, her petticoat. Dr Ghosh explained that this was a form of crystallization of urine, that certain substances in Roo's body were poisoning his urine. In his opinion, neither microsurgery nor removal of the kidneys would work, because both kidneys were losing their ability to function, becoming weaker by the day. The word dialysis cropped up in his diagnosis eventually. For now he gave some medicine for cleansing the urine, each pill costing thirty rupees. He regretfully advised Ishwari to take Roo to Vellore. He liked the boy, the doctor said.

Ishwari left with the prescription and medicine. She went up to the terrace of Dinratri. There she discovered that the rain had entered the room through the open window and soaked the bed. Roo was curled up on this wet bed. She threw her bag and reports on the floor, shook Roo awake and slapped him hard. 'Bastard!' she said. 'Pretending to be ill all day? Couldn't you even get up to shut the window?'

—

A physiotherapist visited Bibaswan at seven every morning, a reiki expert visited on alternate days at nine o'clock. Sometimes Ishwari caught a glimpse of Dr Basak, the famous orthopaedic specialist. He instructed Bibaswan to use crutches rather than walk unaided. His body needed rest. Three of his joints had undergone major surgery, they should not be subjected to any pressure for at least two or three months. Bibaswan told Dr Basak, 'My entire body aches around the clock, Doctor. I can't take it any more.'

'Music, music,' answered Dr Basak. 'It works, I tell

you. Immerse yourself in melody, you'll forget your aches and pains.'

'Is this what you prescribe for everyone these days?'

'Different strokes for different folks.'

One day, after much pleading by Sita, Guru Shibayanchandra stepped into Radheshyam House. He was an Art of Living guru, offering the chance to experience Sri Sri Ravi Shankar's brand of spirituality. The hall was cleared to make arrangements for the guru and the guests. A sandalwood stool was pulled out of the storeroom, Persian carpets were laid out, floating candles and lotus buds were arranged in an enormous brass pot in the middle of the room, beautiful candles and plates of flowers were placed in the corners, sticks of fragrant incense glowed everywhere. Guru Shibayan arrived, dressed in saffron, carrying a golden bowl. His eyes lowered, he informed his followers of beautiful ways of living, accompanied by glorious smiles; one of his disciples went into a trance and began to play the tanpura. Bibaswan sat in a chair, frowning. The catering company silently supervised the process of feeding two hundred people. Halfway through, Bibaswan signalled to Ishwari with his eyes and went upstairs with Sukhendu's and Kalicharan's help. When she joined him a little later, Bibaswan said, 'I couldn't sit there any more, please tell my mother.'

'All right,' she answered. 'Do you need anything?'

'I want music, Ishwari.'

'Should I put on some music?'

'Don't you know how to sing?'

'Only a little. But not ghazals.'

'Never mind then. My ears are tuned to ghazals now.'

'What do I do then?'

'All right, you needn't sing, just read the lines.'

Ishwari proceeded to read, and Bibaswan said, 'This one's set in Madhukosh. I can imagine the tune in my head.'

As she read, salty tears escaped Ishwari's eyes...

Khud ko padta hoon, chhod deta hoon
Ek warq roz mod deta hoon
Kanpte hont, bheegti palkein
Baat adhuri hi chhod deta hoon

I read myself, I give up,
I turn a page every day.
Lips trembling, lashes moist,
I leave it all unsaid.

Bibaswan said, 'Are you crying?' Ishwari nodded. 'Do you like crying?'

'I don't know, Bibaswan.'

Sighing, Bibaswan said, 'I desperately want to cry too, but I can't.'

Ishwari tried to wipe her tears away but Bibaswan said, 'Let them be.' Bibaswan didn't ask even once why she was unhappy, what the tears were for. She couldn't tell him that if Roo had to have surgery, the operation and subsequent costs would add up to eighty thousand rupees, according to Dr Chitrabhanu Ghosh's calculations. 'I want to paint all night tonight,' Bibaswan said, looking at her. 'Tania is absolutely vivid to me today. Every line of her body is clear.'

Ishwari suddenly said, 'Flames have no form, Bibaswan! What shape can this grief have? This is fire. You can paint Tania any way you like, so what if the lines don't map her figure?'

Bibaswan shuddered and went to the balcony. 'You can leave for the day, Ishwari, switch the light off before you go,' he said.

——

Maharaj Pramananda visited Bibaswan for yoga on some evenings. On those days Ishwari left Radhesh-yam House around five. Taking a notebook and pencil out onto the terrace, she made Roo do sums. She asked him, 'Tell me, eight-eight-za?' Roo couldn't answer. He couldn't do sums, he got his English spellings wrong, he nodded off to sleep the moment she made him sit down with books.

'Shouldn't Roo be going to school?' Preeti asked. 'Put him in a school nearby, I'll take him there and bring him back.'

One day Sukul informed her that Preeti was from the red-light district of Kalighat, her mother was a sex worker. Ishwari recoiled at this but Sukul said, 'She wants to get out of that environment, she'll be saved if she can stay here.'

Ishwari called Preeti. 'Why don't you stay here all the time? You can sleep in the attic, no problem.'

Preeti agreed at once, tears rolling down her cheeks. 'Who wants to go back? But if I don't go, they'll create trouble here.'

'I'll manage that,' Sukul declared. 'Stay here.'

Ishwari felt a little more assured about this life on the roof. Preeti loved Roo, she played with him constantly. Ishwari made Preeti do their daily shopping and take the clothes for ironing. She gave her own lunch to Preeti, eating the ten-course meal at Radheshyam House with pleasure. Despite all these efforts, she managed to save very little money for

Roo's treatment. And Bibaswan worried her more and more because he was doing everything possible to recover quickly.

—

When Bibaswan immersed himself in painting, Ishwari had nothing to do with her time. She wanted to pull out a book to read but soon realised that Bibaswan expected her to tilt her head and watch him paint. She was aware that Bibaswan had an artistic pride – his work was quite good too, but she didn't see in him the artist's distance from reality or quest for uncertainty. Bibaswan had imagination but no sense of wonder. He was peculiar, and she found him more and more peculiar with every passing day. Sometimes she liked him, and at other times she found him unbearable. He seemed extremely selfish. There was no specific reason why she thought so. The person in the house behind Dinratri, whom she could only glimpse now and then, shattered her insides into smithereens, made her bleed from her hands and feet, made her unfulfilled desires groan, stimulated her into wanting sex, wanting to be kissed, wanting to moan with pleasure, her arousal hitting her like a spray of pepper on her eyes – but she had no such feeling for Bibaswan, who was very handsome. Bibaswan had been blocked by calculations of gains and losses. She sighed when he gazed at her too long; she was afraid that once he got better she would have to look for another job. She could not look at him the way unattached twenty-seven can look at unattached thirty-eight.

Only last evening, about thirty thousand rupees' worth of paint arrived for Bibaswan from Mumbai. He was testing the colours, painting a thick layer of black on the canvas, as he looked at Ishwari again and again as though she was his subject, while Rashid Khan sang...

Naina bharo kajra sohe
Rasili rangili priyake
Pyari sohavni... manmohan

Line your eyes with black
My enchanting, beautiful lover
You have won my heart.

To dispel her awkwardness, she said, 'How come you're not playing ghazals today?'

'Why don't you dress up, Isha?' Bibaswan asked.

'No need to.'

'Oh, you're so vain. Ma will take you shopping

today. I can't stand this saffron robe of yours any more.'
She lowered her head. Bibaswan declared, 'Ma must
make you wear what I want you to wear.'

Part of the job, she thought. But then things
changed completely. Music, art, watching Eisenstein
all afternoon, caramel custard in the early evening,
fruit jam, arranging roses, changing the lights in the
room in tandem with the change of mood… it was
true that her saffron sari was long past its prime with
all the washing and ironing.

'Rantideb Uncle is visiting this evening,' she said.
'I must to meet him.'

'About what?'

'About my son's illness.'

'I see. My mother probably wants to leave today,
Isha.' Bibaswan put his paintbrush down and went to
the toilet.

Lunchtime followed. Bibaswan usually ate in his
room, requesting Ishwari to join him. She couldn't
eat to her heart's content in his presence. She could
only pick at her food with a spoon. Bibaswan was
a changed man at this time, continuously requesting
her to try the dishes he liked. After eating, they talked
about the significance of ghazals.

'I've listened to ghazals,' said Ishwari, 'but I don't
know much about them.'

Bibaswan said, 'Mahir is coming in May for a day, he'll stay here. He is performing at Nazrul Mancha, and since I can't go, he has promised to sing all night on the balcony for me – an exclusive night of music. You must stay over that night.'

'Is Mahir a friend of yours?'

'Yes. I met him after listening to him sing. We shared a great deal after that. After Tania's death he sang for me nights on end. He is a very nice man.' Bibaswan's expression grew intense. He withdrew within himself again, taking his eyes away from Ishwari.

Ishwari resolved to wash away the sadness clinging to Bibaswan's face – she felt as though she wanted to do some extra work to make up for the next day being a holiday. 'Ghazal is pure poetry, it's not meant to be sung, is it?'

'You're right,' said Bibaswan. 'Ghazal, katayat, rubai, nazm – it's all poetry. They're classifications, like sonnets or rhymes or blank verse or couplets.'

Ishwari got to her feet, looked for Mahir and put his music on.

Yeh aaine se akele guftagu kya hai
Joh main nahi hoon toh tere rubaroo kya hai

What is this private conversation with yourself in
the mirror?
What is there for you to look at when I'm not
with you?

Bibaswan listened with his eyes closed. When he
opened them again, they were red, his nostrils were
flared, and he said, 'The word ghazal means, "from
the lover to the beloved".'

They went out to the balcony and sat down. Ishwari rang for Sukhendu and ordered coffee. Bibaswan
liked his coffee black, she added milk and sugar to
hers. The evening failed to turn to gold in a sky that
held a hint of a storm, the surroundings were sul-
len. Bibaswan said, 'The first two lines of a ghazal are
known as the matla. A sher with the shayar's name in
it is known as the makhta. For instance...

Ret ke ghar bana bana ke
Faraz jaaney kyun khud hi tod deta hoon

I make houses of sand,
Faraz, I don't know why I break them myself.

'Faraz! He is the shayar here. Get it? *Samjhe?*'
Ishwari laughed. 'I got it.'

Bibaswan stroked her cheek, saying, 'Then there was the radif or the kafiya. The syllable of the first line is repeated over and over – that's the radif. In this one, for instance, you have words like 'rubaroo' and 'aarzoo' and 'aabroo' repeatedly. The 'roo' is the radif.'

Roo? Wasn't Roo someone she knew? Ishwari stood up absently. 'Roo' kept appearing repeatedly in her life too. Roo! Her Roo. Like a half-burnt corpse with reedy sticks for limbs. Pebbled eyes, protruding belly – he vomited all the time, he couldn't pass urine. 'It hurts,' he screamed, blood flowed with the urine. And kafiya is the rhythm.

Kya hai, aarzoo kya hai, aabroo kya hai

What is it? Desire? Dignity?

Ishwari left. Bibaswan called out to her, 'Isha, Isha!' Sita saw her too. 'Ishwari? What's wrong?' She could not hear, she forgot to listen – she left Radheshyam House.

Outside, Ishwari took a taxi. The streets seemed empty. Was it because a storm was brewing? She beat the storm to Dinratri. She climbed up the stairs to the roof and found the door to the roof wide open, the lock hanging outside. She was surprised. She assumed the worst. Had Preeti run away with Roo? The very next moment she concluded that no one would run away with Roo. He had no value. What had happened, then? And she discovered the door to the attic unlocked, the door shut from within. She climbed up the spiral staircase silently, and paused for a moment. Then she threw the door open.

Preeti and Sukul. Half undressed. In the act. Sukul's trousers were around his ankles, Preeti had taken off her salwar, and her thin legs were entwined around Sukul as she rocked back and forth. Such a young girl. She already knew so much? Ishwari suddenly remembered that just the other day, the other day... someone had raped Preeti... Ishwari wanted to disappear under the resentment, the misery, the torture, the humiliation. Nikhil Biswas had wrinkled his nose and said, 'so you've hired a whore.' Not even Rantideb Babu would approve.

Ishwari ran downstairs, trembling; Preeti ran to the bathroom; footsteps could be heard on the stairs. Ishwari caught hold of the fleeing Sukul, ripped his shirt off. Her city-educated lips couldn't utter a word. She started slapping Sukul. Faces materialised, asked 'what's the matter, what's the matter.' Grabbing a fistful of his hair, she flung him away from her... And still I try to understand the evolution of this novel. I reflect, yes, it happens, this is just what happens – this is natural – sexuality enters people's lives through any opening it can find. We may not acknowledge it, but wherever we end up these are the scenes that leap out at us when the window is suddenly opened. A cloying, sticky mass. That pavement, that house at the back, Sukul and I, Preeti and Sukul, Dinratri, Biba-swan and I, and I and he. And he is everything. This he himself is existence.

This he himself is existence.

He is the current that takes us from existence to non-existence. He is the one who ceaselessly bears aloft the burden of the non-existence of our existence, saying, when the sky, the air, the water, the earth, all of it is wiped out from our sight, when the tornado blinds us, that is the precise moment when existence is produced from the formlessness of non-existence.

But my novel? Written and then burned? Neither existence nor non-existence. But does the non-exist-ence allow me to forget its existence? Isn't it fighting continuously, isn't it still blazing in conflict? And in this war between existence and non-existence is born enormous power, enormous pressure. A dense, continuously exploding, super-sentient being, dis-connected from space, from time, with no restraint left to exercise, no possibility of return. A return that would have included Preeti, Sukul – and even me.

Ishwari asked everyone to leave the terrace and told the sobbing Preeti, 'Go downstairs, take a bath,' and opened the door in search of her son.

—

Ishwari remained in bed, holding Roo close. It was completely dark, not a light had been switched on in the terrace or the room. Somewhere Preeti was weeping quietly. Roo had gone to sleep with his hand on Ishwari's breast – she thought of getting out of bed, but each time she drew Roo a little closer to herself. She guarded Roo as though there was no end to this. Someone was hammering on the door to the roof.

Preeti entered and switched on the light. 'Someone's here to see you, he's waiting downstairs. Montu gave this for you.' Preeti's voice was hoarse, she still couldn't understand why Ishwari had behaved in such contrary fashion. Why hadn't she scolded her?

Ishwari unfolded the slip.

You have to come, Ishwari... right now. Bib.

Was Bibaswan here? She ran downstairs. No, it was Monotosh, the driver. She went back upstairs to lock the door to the roof, and then got into the car.

The large chandelier in the hall of Radheshyam House glittered, there were lights in the corners, lamps whose beams fell on the paintings – but Bibaswan's room was dark, only the lamp on his desk was shining. Once her eyes had adjusted to the darkness, she approached the sofa where he was sitting almost in silence, and touched his crutch. Bibaswan stood up when he sensed her presence. He seemed agitated, he tried twice to grip his crutch and failed both times. His left hand dug into her shoulder. 'I can throw you out, Isha,' he said.

Ishwari found his eyes. 'Why?' she asked.

'Why?' Bibaswan was taken aback. 'Because you insulted art. Do you understand?'

'Art? Art means nothing to me.'

'Nothing? Music, art, literature – is all this nothing?'

'Nothing. To me art is something you don't yourself understand and therefore don't allow others to understand. Art means destroying the opportunities, the scope, the freedom to understand. It means killing the momentum of an energy that covers all of space. To me art is non-existence. I want to leave, Bibaswan, I want to go back to my son.'

Bibaswan let go of her shoulder to grasp her waist with such force that she thought his fingers would pierce her stomach. Her breasts brushed against his chest, the darkness emphasised their shape. Her chin touched Bibaswan's face and he rubbed his hardened jaw against Ishwari's cheeks, her neck, her shoulders.

'Don't come here again if you can't acknowledge art,' Bibaswan said.

She laughed. 'Acknowledge? Be an instrument of art?' She burst into tears.

'I repeat, Isha. I cannot leave you. I want to get inside you.'

'Like an art critic? They're even more horrifying than the flames in which my novel was burned.'

'Shut up.'

'They're horrifying because each of them wanted to be an artist but became a critic instead.'

'Fold your wings, Isha.'

Bibaswan's warm tongue touched her earlobes, the corner of her lips. It tasted her nose, moistened her eyelids. She wept uncontrollably, 'I've promised to tell him a story, Bibaswan.'

'A little longer, a little more, Isha. Let me hurt you once. Let me push some pain into you. Let me cast some pain over you.'

'No. I shall go to Roo now.'

'Then why did you come, Isha? Tell me, why did you come?' Ishwari could offer no answer, all her learning seemed to have left her. Her novel, full of imbalance, fell into conflict, with one of the three – language, subject and form – falling behind.

'One kiss,' said Bibaswan, 'and then you may leave.'

—

Since Ishwari and I are two distinct beings, different in terms of substance, this novel can be understood if we disobey each other, betray each other. But when Ishwari and I become one, when the tiny currents and canals and cascades within us mingle, the atlas of our soul changes and this unseemly disparity between 'Ishwari' and 'I' is dissolved.

Standing before the discoloured mirror in Dinratri, Ishwari had asked herself, 'Why should I fight pleasure?' And since love was the simplest route to pleasure, Ishwari had fallen in love with Bibaswan over several rounds. At least, she had wanted to. That was why she had wrung out all her sensations to talk to him on the phone with rapt attention while waiting with Roo in the corridor of the government hospital. Bibaswan had given her the phone – a small instrument that could be folded, complete with a working connection. 'I want to be connected with you all the time, Isha,' he had told her. Bibaswan had pinched Ishwari's lips with his fingertips and kissed them, while her groin, still clothed, had rubbed against something as hard as Shiva's phallus. Biting her lip, she shook her head and smiled, and since then they had been talking continuously on the phone. She entered Radheshyam House listening to his voice on the receiver, and she dialled his number the moment she left. Even after her return to Dinratri their conversation did not end. Bibaswan said, 'See what Keki Daruwalla has said, Isha...'

> The feel of water over rounded stone
> Like your hand over
> The beloved's hips and thigh

'Naughty boy!' she laughed, falling onto her bed on her stomach, her head dangling over the side, her thick hair sweeping down to the floor like rain, covering her face so she could not see Roo sitting quietly at the window with his plate of rice and boiled potato. Roo called out to her several times, trying to say something. 'Wait,' Ishwari signalled. And then she was drunk with poetry – with poetry, love, melody, colour, friendship, love, abjection, slavery.

They spoke through the night, and now she felt terribly sleepy on those nights when Roo's drums of pain beat the loudest. She felt as though a toxic smoke emanated from his tiny frame, making her body and senses droop with heaviness. Othwerise Ishwari could go on talking with the phone pressed to her ear...

She could no longer afford to consult Chitrabhanu Ghosh. She couldn't afford his four-hundred rupee fee. She felt embarrassed among the crowd of people on the benches in the government hospital. Embarrassed, because Bibaswan was whispering to her, 'Tomorrow? Tomorrow, Isha?'

—

A mangy dog sat near Roo's feet, half its ear torn off. It was gasping for breath. The dog would die any minute. Roo was observing it carefully. Ishwari was carrying a bottle of glucose water for Roo – when he collapsed he had to be given concentrated glucose water. Grabbing the bottle from her, Roo poured a little out on the floor. Gasping, the dog lapped it up. Ishwari watched but didn't say anything, she had devoted herself body and soul to listening to Bibaswan.

He was saying, 'Come right now, Ishwari. It's past one, aren't you having lunch with me?'

'Of course I am, please wait a bit. I'll be there.'

'I feel very lonely, Ishwari, I feel lonely these days without you, like I used to as a child, when my mother died and my father sent me to boarding school, or those days after Tania's death, or when I felt I would go mad in Maryland all by myself…'

She wanted to cry. 'I won't let you be alone any more, Bibaswan, I will be with you all the time,' she said, as though he was her only source of unhappiness now.

'When you're with me, I hear Tania's breath in this room.'

It made her miserable, but she said, 'You love Tania very much, don't you?'

'Very much.'

'And don't you remember the baby?'

'Don't remind me, don't. I'll go mad.'

'Look for him in other children, Bibaswan.'

He fell silent at this. Ishwari became cautious. You can look for your woman in other women, but does your child exist in other children? Does your ego rest in your own child?

Seeing that the outpatient department was being closed, she rose to her feet and said, 'What's the matter, isn't the doctor seeing any more patients?'

'No, it's two o'clock. Closing for the day.'

'But I have a ticket, I've been waiting such a long time.' An angry nurse poked her head out of a window. 'Seven times I called out his name, Mahiruho,

Mahiruho. You couldn't hear. You were talking on the phone. Keep talking!'

She stood holding Roo's hand, wishing her tall frame would waste away, just like this filthy, sick environment, this use of subaltern language, this gathering of the poor, the destitute, the cats and dogs and cleaners. The same nurse said, 'Who's this? Your son? Bleeding when you pee? Go home, boy. Forget about seeing the doctor.'

Ishwari asked dispiritedly, 'Will this ticket be valid tomorrow?'

She heard the piercing voice of the nurse, 'Why don't you talk on the phone some more.'

When Ishwari took Roo back to Dinratri, Preeti said with her head bowed, 'We're out of cooking gas, Didi.' Preeti couldn't look her in the eye any more.

'I'll phone Sukul,' she said. Preeti looked at her, startled.

Ishwari left as soon as she had given Roo his medicine. She went directly to Kalighat and found Sukul without any effort. Entering the taxi, she said without wasting words, 'Hastings!' When the taxi began to move, she told Sukul about running out of gas.

'I'll get you a cylinder,' said Sukul. After a while he asked, 'Have you thrown Preeti out?'

She burst into tears then. 'Sukul, what about Roo?

You haven't asked about Roo even once. Didn't you ever love Roo even a little bit? Tell me?'

'I used to visit because of you,' Sukul said.

—

Bibaswan was in bed. Just as Ishwari had seen him that first day – asleep. She hadn't seen him the same way again in the past month and a half.

'Bibaswan is an introvert,' Rantideb had said. Once or twice in the early days, Ishwari had sensed as much from Bibaswan's behaviour. Then he began to talk to her endlessly.

The stern lines of impatience disappeared from his expression. In fact he let his guard down so completely before Ishwari that when he was in pain from the wounds on his back and ribs, he groaned loudly without embarrassment. Sita had told her to use the room next door if she needed to but Bibaswan didn't give her the opportunity to step in there. He only tied her down. Over the past month and a half, Ishwari had savoured this love, this eagerness, with every pore in her body, till her wonder dissipated gradually and she grew accustomed to it.

As soon as Ishwari entered the room, she asked Bibaswan, 'Have you had lunch?'

'No,' answered Bibaswan.

'Nor have I, let's eat.'

'I don't want lunch, you go and eat.'

'Why? Are you angry?'

'You are so late.'

The room was extremely cold compared to the heat outside. This was how Bibaswan liked it. Soon she felt cool and fresh. Sitting down on the sofa, she said, 'I took Roo to the government hospital. You know what it's like.'

'No, I don't know, and I don't want to know either. How will it help me to know? It's the same everywhere, what can I do about it?'

'Haven't you ever been curious about what's wrong with Roo, Bibaswan? You never ask me about my struggles with him. You have no idea how alone Roo and I are.'

Bibaswan sat up on his bed. 'I know, Isha. I have discussed this with Rantideb Uncle, we have been wondering how to help. But we don't have a solution to every problem, do we? Moreover, we are not to blame for what is happening to you.'

She sat in silence, then said, 'I'll be late tomorrow too, Bibaswan.'

'Why?'

'I have to go to the hospital again.'

'And what will I do?'

'Can't you manage for a bit?'

'How? Don't you see, I need someone? I need you, Isha.' Bibaswan made this last statement so fervently that it sounded new to Ishwari.

Billowing like a monsoon cloud, she went to Bibaswan, 'Shall I tell Sukhendu to bring your lunch?'

Bibaswan got to his feet, supporting himself on his crutch, and walked up to the easel. 'Come here,' he said. 'Did you see this? Have you even noticed what I've been painting this past week?'

Ishwari went around the easel to look at the canvas, surprised to see herself. Bibaswan had painted her. The portrait wasn't complete but Ishwari could see herself. She was drowning in thick clusters of roses, holding her hand out to someone. She was nude. Ishwari embraced Bibaswan, asking, 'Have you ever seen me this way?'

'Not with my eyes, but I have felt you this way with my hands, Isha.'

'Why so many roses, Bibaswan?'

'Roses have the scent of sex, didn't you know? I want to have a lot of sex with you, Ishwari. I'll take you all night, all day, then I'll paint, and then have sex again – I'll read poetry with your body in a delirium.'

Held in a firm embrace by Bibaswan, Ishwari said, 'A poem, Bibaswan, a poem. Want to hear it?'

Exploring Ishwari's lips with his, Bibaswan said, 'I do.'

Bibaswan smiled after she had whispered the lines in his ear. 'All right, not sex – love. I want to make love to you. All right?' Slowly, he released her. 'I know you're angry with me, and I know the reason for your disappointment. I feel sorry for you.'

She said, 'I feel sorry for you too, Bibaswan. You still cannot paint Tania without seeing her.'

—

Is this what one calls a love–hate relationship? I have developed a relationship with Bibaswan but can it be called love? Do I love Bibaswan? If I do, why do I look into the room in the house behind ours as soon as I'm back at Dinratri? Why do I feel miserable when the room is dark and the door closed? And why am I wracked by pleasure when the room is lit up? This is the only unmixed joy in my life now, seeing 'him'. I am different when I see him. A cascade of coffee-coloured hair flows down my back, my eyes become taut, my lips warm, my spine rears up like a snake. My breasts grow into laden waves with every breath. My buttocks and thighs become aroused and alert, as though he has been following me for a long time and we have suddenly come face to face. And

I do come face to face with him one day – in the supermarket inside the petrol pump next to Dinratri. I'm trying to exit through its glass doors when he comes in. His arm almost touches mine and I immediately know which brand of cologne he uses. After exiting I return to the shop and rummage through the shelves, watching him. Not exactly him, but his reflection in the mirror. He watches me too, but it doesn't seem like he has seen me before. He likes the way I look in the jeans and pastel-coloured kurta that Sita has given me. He watches me through narrowed eyes, pays for the frozen food, pays for the cigarettes – I leave, so does he. I enter Dinratri, his eyes following me. He sees me enter, he thinks I must be a boarder.

Up on the roof, I wait by the window. Some time later he appears on the balcony and lights a cigarette. 'Preeti, come here,' I call out loudly. Startled, he turns around. Something occurs to him and he frowns, then smiles covertly. He looks incredible in this setting. A thief of hearts. A current of youth in black trackpants and white T-shirt. Fair, six feet tall, closely cropped hair. He looks at me uninhibitedly while he smokes. When Preeti appears I tell her to buy some rice. 'Measure it out when you cook it,' I remind her. I am enveloped in a marvellous feeling, my insides glow. I wonder, does he have no one either? Like me,

no love to make him soar? Does he only have someone to kiss him? I want to know, I want to know
everything.

The book with which Roo had waited for me on
the secret road, *The Adventures of Don Quixote*, is now
tattered from all the times it has been read and han-
dled. As I am about to leave, Roo comes up to me
and asks, 'Will you buy me another storybook, Ma?'
Roo is bold enough to call me 'Ma' after a very long
time.

'I will,' I agree. 'The next time we visit the doctor.
Okay?'

—

Bibaswan is pleased to see me. 'You look glamorous,'
he says.

Forgetting my past and present, I laugh.

I recognise my submissive love for Bibaswan and
his recalcitrant emotions for me – while talking to
Bibaswan on the phone, I think of 'him', but eventually it's Bibaswan I go back to. I have to return to my
love-hate relationship, I have to accept the envelope
from Bibaswan's drawer, I have to bear the heat of his
caresses.

—

I know 'he' left after we met the other day. The room is dark. He returns after three or four days. He stands on his balcony, smoking a cigarette. I am running late for Roo's hospital appointment. I am supposed to confirm the date of the surgery today, schedule a CT scan, I have to wait in a long queue – despite all this I do not leave.

He signals a question: 'Who are you?'

I shrug, 'I'm me.'

He signals, 'No name?'

'You want to know?'

We both went downstairs, onto the road and into the supermarket. Fiddling with tubes of shaving cream and toothpaste in front of the mirror, he asks again, 'Who are you?'

'I'm Ishwari.'

'You stay on the rooftop?' I nod.

'Strange,' he says. 'Alone?'

'No.'

'Married?'

'Divorced.'

'Oh, I'm sorry. How long will you be here?'

'As long as possible.'

'Can we meet some time? I'd like to talk to you.'

'I don't know your name.'

'I'll tell you when we meet. Meet me today?'

'Today? No, I can't, today.'

'Why?'

'I have to take my son to the doctor. He's very ill, he's been bedridden for a long time. He'll have surgery soon. A major operation.'

Examining a can of shaving foam with great attention, he says, 'You have a son?'

'Yes.'

'Okay.' He tosses the can up in the air and catches it. 'All right, no problem. I'll see you later.'

'Tomorrow?'

'Some other time. I don't live here, I'm busy. Anyway, I have to go. Take care. Take care of your son. Bye.'

He appears again. I stand at the window when I see the light go on in the room, my hair flows down my back, my breasts heavy... He appears on his verandah, glances at the window, and doesn't recognise me. He turns away in search of other sights.

—

They found a lump in Roo's bladder. The lump was growing slowly. There were drops of blood in the bathroom on the roof. In the past three months, Roo had eaten nothing but rice, gruel, mashed potato and papaya – he had drunk only glucose water. He couldn't even get out of bed and make it as far as the window any more. Preeti carried him to the bathroom. The other day, he stood up suddenly while they were waiting in the corridor at the Institute of Child Health Care. Four or five children were playing close by, Roo went up to them. Ishwari couldn't make out what they said but she saw one of them tug at his arm, wherein Roo slumped to the floor without effort and passed out.

Two Muslim women helped Ishwari a great deal that day. After the doctor had examined Roo she quickly brought him back to Dinratri.

'His blood pressure has dropped,' the doctor had said. 'You've decided to keep him at home but this is a life-threatening condition, something could happen anytime. He should be in hospital. Besides, this constant pain around the waist means it's getting worse. No one knows how long he's been carrying these stones. You say you haven't seen him for almost a year, and the child can't communicate his symptoms. What can we do in this situation? If the stones persist, the kidneys have to be removed – because they're damaged, they don't function.'

But even this conversation took place a month ago. Ever since the lump was diagnosed, there was a new silence in the doctors' comportment. Roo's physical condition did not permit surgery right now, they said. The surgery was cancelled, Ishwari brought Roo back home.

Ishwari had been thinking about Roo all this time. As his health worsened, Bibaswan recovered. Bibaswan walked on his own. He didn't want to stay in Kolkata much longer. He wanted to move to Bangalore and settle there. The suppressed anxiety in Radheshyam House over Bibaswan's fitness had largely been dispelled. Everyone wanted Bibaswan to drive to the club and walk about with Ishwari by his side. But Bibaswan wanted more time. Everyone was happy with that too. Let Bibaswan do things his way. It was enough for the family that he had managed to overcome his grief for Tania to a great extent. Even Umapati admitted that it was Ishwari who was responsible for Bibaswan's return to normalcy in most ways.

She had no idea which of the two – her going to work for Bibaswan with the intensity and perseverance of a deep-sea diver, or her floating relationship with him, thrashing about on the surface – would eventually prevail. She still talked with him. She told him stories, stories with appropriate settings and characters. She arranged flowers, trimmed the dead leaves of the fern on the balcony. Poetry made them desperate sometimes – Bibaswan rubbed his face on her stomach, Ishwari lay there like carbon. She realised now that she had no sex drive any more, though she wanted to live. Bibaswan still tried to paint Tania frequently. She felt no unhappiness at this. But when Bibaswan told her about the flat in Bangalore, the south-facing eighth-floor flat, from where planes could be seen taking off and landing, something changed inside her and she wished she could cup Roo's raised face in her palms and say, 'Roo. You have to give me up.' She wished she could say, 'I want to live, Roo, just like you do. Perhaps I'll get a job, maybe I'll find a place to stay, but what does a job and a place to stay have to do with living? To live is to live within a relationship, to live with someone I can relate to. I cannot relate to you, I cannot.'

One day Ishwari decided she would say all this and telephone those who had a claim to Roo. She would telephone the person who had once told her that a wife is the most expensive prostitute, the person who used to beat her, have sex with her and then beat her again. She telephoned but the phone rang and rang – no one answered to relieve her. She made enquiries and discovered that no one was waiting there for Roo. They had moved. She wanted to weep, she felt as though she had been cheated, cheated badly.

—

The day Gourohori was admitted to hospital with a raging fever, Bibaswan insisted on making love to Ishwari wantonly. He wanted to lose all equilibrium and roll into the tunnel with her. And indeed the shower curtain snapped, pitching both of them into the bathtub. Ishwari was shaken by the sound of their fall. 'Sita Aunty is at home, Bibaswan. Someone may come. I've asked Sukhendu to bring your soup.'

'Who cares,' answered Bibaswan. 'Let them come. I'm handicapped. I overbalanced and fell on top of you.'

Embarrassed, Ishwari extricated herself. Getting to her feet, she helped Bibaswan up. He cupped her cheek with his huge paw. 'Do I trouble you a lot, Isha?'

'No, not at all,' she answered absently.

'Isha!'

She looked at herself in the mirror, not noticing when Bibaswan went out of the bathroom. He sounded angry, disappointed. Seconds later, when she registered this, she ran to him. 'What is it? Why are you angry?'

'You don't pay attention to me, Ishwari. The work you do is hardly anything. Even if I put that aside, you don't feel any love or affection or compassion for me. You only come here for the envelope. I'm no one to you – just a support system for you and your son.'

Ishwari sat down near his feet, covering her face with her hands. 'Gourohori Babu is in hospital, Bibaswan, that's why I'm a little distracted.'

'No, Isha, don't play tricks with me any more. Let's talk straight. Everyone knows your son is ill, everyone's sympathetic towards you, we're human beings too. I myself was about to die some months ago, I know what life is, how valuable it is – but are your feelings for me even a fraction of what I feel for you? Do you understand what I want? Do you understand what I need, what I seek from you like a madman? I'm human, I'm flesh and blood. You cannot tackle me with words alone. And you believe in nothing but words. Poetry, music, fantasy – but for how long, Isha? To me your words are stillborn, lifeless creatures. Please undress your words, unclothe yourself. I want to have you like a good, mindless girl who will give me everything without questions, without doubts.'

'Your experience of love is not the same as mine, Bibaswan,' said Ishwari. 'The way you want me, the way you want Tania, the way you are still aroused at the thought of Tania's body and are able to combine her with me, the way you say that even if the colours of the rainbow were to change, the beauty of the blue sky would depend on itself, is not something I can understand. I want you too, Bibaswan, but like a forbidden fruit, I want you while I set myself aside.'

'You're playing with words again, Ishwari.'

'No, Bibaswan, when a singer sings it is true that he sings, but he cannot recognise his own voice right away. Only after years of practice does he know what his voice really is. Our everyday life is a quest for this voice. I'm looking for the voice in which I can express myself to you, reveal myself to you.'

'Is it so difficult to accept me, Isha?'

'I love you, Bibaswan. What else do I have but this relationship?'

'Get rid of your child,' said Bibaswan. 'I don't want anyone coming between us.'

After twilight turned into evening, just as Ishwari was thinking of leaving to see Gourohori, Bibaswan blocked her way, saying, 'Tell me this instant about all your experiences with love. I want to know the points of difference between your love and mine. Why won't you allow the strings of doubt and unwillingness to be loosened in any circumstance? Why, why do you think that all your dreams are becoming an embodiment of life – under the pressure and heat and tears and contamination of carrying the burden of your individuality, of your existence? Why, Isha?'

They had called this job of hers friendship. Ishwari knew she was not fit for any manner of friendship, and that all friendships were impermanent. But she knew her job, she knew the life spring of her assignment, and so she began to tell stories, stories with consistent characters and settings. She told a story of her love for a sailor. A sailor was once her lover. She met him while on the run in Mumbai – they sailed the seas together and got married on the Arab coast.

Ishwari had not told Rantideb this story, nor Gourohori, nor Sukul – she had heard the story from a woman she had met on a train. The story was about this woman's life. She had shown Ishwari her skin, rotted and shrivelled from burns. Because this novel is one of truths and lies, and any novel is one of truths and lies, any story has the potential to become another's life story. Ishwari saw nothing wrong with telling Bibaswan this story now.

'My sailor's name was Segun. He would tell me that he loved me, and I believed him. His love was my only anchor in that alien environment, amid the continuous roiling and pitching of the stormy ocean. Segun was a supremely arrogant man, extremely combative. He would be lost in the maze of the ship all day, while I remained in my cabin, and at night he would return drunk. But I had no aversion to this floating life. What possible attraction could the land hold for someone who had no one ashore, no bonds, no relationships? There was a white staircase next to our cabin, which took you to the fifth deck. Every night Segun would make me undress on the fifth deck.'

Ishwari continued, no longer remembering exactly what the woman on the train had told her. 'Segun, my sailor, my man, would place me on the deck under that sky. I would contort myself in a way that made my vagina thrust upwards, the stars nestling in the sky took a glimpse of my genitals. They would see it weep. I would lie on my back and Segun would insert not his own organ, but Japanese toys. They would whirl inside me, rotating and vibrating madly. After kneading me all night he would put away the toys in his bag and go down the white stairs, and I would lie in a pool of alcohol and my own blood. No one knew how long I would remain unconscious, on the other side of sleep, under the wind on the fifth deck.' When Ishwari got to this point, she bit her tongue sharply after it got entangled in her teeth. Blood spurted out at once. Still limping, Bibaswan rushed to fetch a towel. His golden-brown Turkish towel gradually soaked up her blood.

What happened to Ishwari is just what happens when the storyteller bites her tongue or the writer's mind dries up. She began to weep uncontrollably. Ishwari's relationship with her mind, where her stories were born, was actually like the one between the novelist and her abandoned novel, or between bedbugs and rotting flesh. And because of this, when Bibaswan kissed Ishwari to suck the blood oozing from her tongue and mouth, her temples began to throb. Giving herself up to Bibaswan's seed, she tried to tell herself as she writhed ferociously that this was work too – it was work – it was work.

'Are you all right, Ishwari?'

'Bibaswan, Bibaswan… Segun, my Segun beat me every day and tried to take me to the fifth deck. He threatened to throw me overboard. He dangled me over the iron railing and poured alcohol down my throat. It gurgled down the path my first lover had described as the golden gate…'

Bibaswan clamped his hand over her mouth. 'Quiet, Ishwari. I don't want to hear any more.'

'No, listen…' Bibaswan shook his head vehemently. She pleaded, 'No, Bibaswan, let me finish.'

Bibaswan moved her hair away from her face. Spreading a towel on her neck, he supported her on his arms like a hangar.

Ishwari said, 'Segun kept me locked up in a cabin for days on end. He wouldn't let me out. Whenever the ship dropped anchor for two or three days, he picked up other women. One day Segun beat me up mercilessly, made furious love to me, wept hysterically, and then left the ship forever. Segun committed suicide, Bibaswan. Breaking his relationship with me, with the ship, he killed himself. He left me alone. I had no one to call my own on the ship. After a seventy-day voyage I floated back to the coast of the Arabian Sea. No one on water, no one on land, no income, no shelter – I wandered around on the streets of Mumbai.'

—

At almost ten at night, when Ishwari had collected herself, splashed water on her face and reached her hand to the door, Bibaswan said, 'So no man has come into your life, Ishwari, whom you can talk about without your voice being robbed of love or desire, without it turning as sharp and bristly as a scorpion?'

Ishwari smiled. 'I have a lover,' she said. 'His name is Salvador Dalí.'

She had barely left the house when she got a text message from Bibaswan: 'You have everything, Ishwari, all you need is love.'

The rest of the way home, Ishwari felt this statement become more and more intense in her heart. And this was the only point at which neither Ishwari nor I had any influence on this novel.

—

Bibaswan's younger sister Sharanya had given Ishwari a large slab of dark chocolate in the morning. She had returned from her summer vacation in Europe a few days ago. Tomorrow she would go back to Bangalore, where she studied. Ishwari put the chocolate bar in her bag. She looked at it when she opened her bag to pay the bus fare. How happy she would have been with the chocolate had Roo been a healthy child. She would run to him after she got back from work, take him in her arms and give him the chocolate. Roo would stuff it into his mouth, leaving smears all over his face. At first Ishwari considered throwing away the chocolate. Then she remembered, 'all you need is love.' She frowned and proceeded to eat the chocolate in the bus with great urgency.

She had spent the day in an air-conditioned house, ate delicious meals, had pleasant conversations, but still she felt exhausted when she reached Dinratri at ten-thirty at night. She asked Prabir how Gourohori was. 'Not very well,' Prabir answered carelessly.

When she stepped onto the terrace, Preeti said, 'Why didn't you phone even once today, Didi?'

She was taken aback. 'That's true, I didn't. But why do you ask?'

'Roo has a stomach ache and has been throwing up since the afternoon. If you don't take him to the doctor this instant he won't survive.' Sitting on her haunches, Preeti began to weep. 'I've been expecting Roo to die any moment. Only I know how I felt all day. There was no one here. If only I could have phoned you, but I couldn't go out and the phone downstairs was locked. Roo was vomiting continuously. I can't take it any more, I'm going to fall ill myself now.'

Ishwari entered the room slowly, without hurrying. Roo, not Roo – no one, actually – lay on the bed. His chest was heaving. The rest of his body was still. She called Preeti. 'What did Roo eat today?'

Preeti snarled in reply, 'What do you suppose? How well stocked is your larder? What could he have eaten besides daal and rice? Is there any meat here? Or fish? How does the question of eating anything else even arise?'

'He must have had something that's making him vomit.'

'I don't know. Why can't you take him to the doctor?'

'Don't cry, tell me whether anything came up when he was retching.'

'You eat nice things all the time! Can't you get an egg roll for me sometimes? He may be ill but I'm not.'

'Don't you know how much money I need for Roo's surgery, Preeti? Don't you know how much the medicines cost every month?'

'Did you bother to give me a new dress for the new year?'

'I didn't know I should have.'

'They give you so many things where you work.'

'They wouldn't be able to talk to me nicely if they didn't – that's why they do, Preeti.'

'It's just that no one will give me a job because my mother's a whore, or I would have quit this job long ago. Who wants to spend all day with a sick child? At least he used to visit me, but you stopped that too.'

'He? Meaning Sukul?'

Preeti turned towards the wall. 'I got some chana-chur on my way back from the market, then I went downstairs for a bath. When I came back I found Roo had finished it.'

She touched Roo's forehead, it was stone cold. Ishwari went to the terrace. A new pharmacy had opened across the road, it hadn't closed for the day yet. She bought medicine and convinced the pharmacist to come back with her to give Roo an injection.

Roo took nearly an hour and a half to fall asleep. Even when his breathing had almost returned to normal, tears streamed from her eyes. At that moment a text message arrived with a beep on her mobile: 'You deserve a better life, Isha. A new life.'

Going out to the terrace, she saw Preeti gazing silently at the sky.

—

Ishwari sensed the bustle as soon as she entered Radheshyam House. She knew Mahir would arrive today. Bibaswan had been bubbling with anticipation at the prospect of meeting him. 'You must wear a sari tomorrow, Isha,' he had told her. It was incredibly hot. She had put on a sari the colour of magnolias, chosen by Sita, with subtle chikan patterns in the Lucknow style. She had worn her hair up in a loose bun, put on brown lipstick and then dabbed most of it off. She had bought four magnolias from the florist near the auto-rickshaw stand and tucked them around the bun. They peeped out of her hair, making her look like a West Asian woman in a sari. Whenever she stood before the mirror, Ishwari was aware of the justification of Sakshi's mother's deep suspicion that she had Muslim blood.

She knocked on Bibaswan's door. 'Yes?' he responded. Turning the knob, she opened the door and a smile spread across Bibaswan's face when he saw her. 'Come, Isha,' he said.

Bibaswan stood up, so did Mahir. Bibaswan said, 'Mahir, meet my friend Ishwari – though we disagree on almost everything. And Isha, introducing Mahir is beyond me, at the most I can only state that I'm a great devotee of his music.'

Mahir said, 'That's who you are, Bibaswan, not who I am.' The three of them laughed.

'Your Bengali is perfect,' said Ishwari.

'My wife is Bengali, you see. Bengali women love to be pampered and there's no better language than Bengali to pamper someone with. That's why I've had to make the effort to learn it.'

Ishwari laughed. Such a big star, but he didn't seem at all conceited. Ishwari had watched Mahir perform in Mumbai. He was a different man on stage, an extraordinary presence. His dreamy eyes radiated brilliance.

Bibaswan said, 'Isha and I have listened to your music together for hours on end.'

Mahir smiled. To Bibaswan he said, 'When will you start going out again?'

'Not so long as I have the slightest limp,' answered

Bibaswan. 'Don't you know they drilled through the bone in my leg to keep it suspended in traction for three months? The hole they drilled hasn't closed yet.'

Mahir gazed at him compassionately and asked, 'Are you painting Tania, Bibaswan?'

'No.' Bibaswan shook his head. 'I've painted one portrait of Isha's, now I'm painting another.'

Mahir raised his eyebrows. 'You're not forgetting something, are you?'

'Uh-huh, Ishwari doesn't even care for me. She has a lover. His name is Salvador Dalí.'

'What!' Mahir exclaimed.

'Not the one you think,' said Bibaswan. 'This Dalí sells pork in Mumbai.'

Ishwari pretended to scold Bibaswan. 'So jealous!' Mahir laughed.

A little later Bibaswan said, 'Ring the bell for Sukhendu, Isha. I want some coffee.'

'I'll get it,' she said.

Ishwari went down to the dining hall. Sita was eating something, and she asked Ishwari to sit down next to her. Ishwari asked Umapati for the coffee and then sat down.

'Bubu's very happy, isn't he, Ishwari?' Sita asked. Ishwari nodded.

Sita spread a thick layer of butter on the bread, followed by a layer of peanut butter, after which she held the jar of honey upside down and moved it around in a circle over the slice of bread before offering it to Ishwari. Ishwari accepted it and thanked her. Sita said, 'I have to go out for a while, please take care of them at lunch, Ishwari.'

'Of course.'

'Umapati has made dalcha. It's delicious, but so spicy I can't touch it. Mahir will love it.' Sita added loudly, 'Umapati, don't forget the papad. There's some pineapple pickle in the cabinet, Ishwari, you could give them some. Add some pepper to the parathas, Umapati.'

Dates, raisins, chunks of mutton, daal, coriander leaves, ghee, chillies – Ishwari knew the ingredients of dalcha. The thought of how delicious it would be when Umapati prepared it made her wistful. If she were to take back some paratha and mutton for Preeti, would Preeti think Ishwari had become hopelessly dependent on her?

Sita continued, 'I'll try my best to be back by two. With such a famous artiste as my guest, I don't feel like going out at all but I don't have a choice. Thank goodness you're here, Ishwari. Wouldn't you agree that a dining table looks graceless without the presence of the women of the house?' Sita put a slice of mango on Ishwari's plate.

Ishwari was no longer embarrassed to eat here. She ate anything she liked in Bibaswan's presence – sometimes he could tell from her expression what she was craving, ice-cream or mousse. The servants followed her orders. Once, Budhaditya returned to Radheshyam for a few days after a fortnight in Delhi; at the same time Sita had to rush off to Canada to console her daughter Sahana, who was feeling miserable. Just as Budhaditya came back, the house brimmed with guests – those who had been invited and those who were calling in on Bibaswan. Ishwari had to take care of many things during those two days. Budhaditya heaped such lavish praise on Ishwari when he left that even Bibaswan raised his eyebrows and said, 'I never imagined my father could say so much without uttering the words "section so-and-so", "serial number such-and-such", "judgement delivered by so-and-so".'

Wiping her mouth with her napkin, Sita said, 'Bubu is going to Santiniketan with Mahir on Saturday. They'll stay there for two or three days. You needn't come during that time.' Then she shrugged. 'But I don't know, you'd better ask Bubu what would be best.'

She thought how wonderful it would be if she

didn't have to go to work for two or three days. And she remembered Roo. It had been a long time since she had showered Roo with her love or tucked him into bed. They slept on the same bed at night, side by side, but she no longer drew Roo to herself. He had become so inert that he lay all night in the same position. Sometimes he seemed so still that she had to shake him to check whether he was dead or alive.

By now Ishwari had realised that the relationship between Sita and Bibaswan was merely a functional one. There was no emotional connection here, Bibaswan was obstinate and Sita extremely intelligent. Whenever there was a conflict with Bibaswan she always yielded, he always got his way. Ishwari didn't offer an elaborate response to Sita, she merely said, 'Yes, Aunty, I'll find out.'

'Kasturi arrives tomorrow. She's going to Santiniketan with them' Sita told her.

Kasturi had come from Hyderabad three or four times in the past few months to meet Bibaswan. As soon as she arrived she gathered Bibaswan at her breast and Bibaswan ran his fingers through her hair. Kasturi and Tania used to be very close friends. When she was here, Bibaswan usually phoned Ishwari to say there was no need for her to come that day.

After telling Sukhendu to take the coffee tray

upstairs, Ishwari told Sita, 'I'd better pack Bibaswan's things right away.'

'Yes, medicines, hot-water bottle… make sure you remember to put in everything he needs.'

—

When she entered the room, she found Bibaswan and Mahir lost in conversation. The windows were closed and the fawn-coloured curtains drawn, the air-conditioner was switched on. An electronic tanpura was laid out on the bed. A sequence of four notes played on it, flitting about the room like butterflies. All the jocularity had been wiped off Mahir's expression, replaced by the discipline of the expert musician. Bibaswan was looking as uncomplicated as a child, as attentive as a student, as penniless as a connossieur – penniless, for he would fill his coffers from the creator and master seated before him.

Ishwari had never seen this Bibaswan. She told Sukhendu to leave and silently made the coffee, served the two men, and sat next to Bibaswan. She had been mistaken. She had been wrong to consider Biba-swan selfish, heartless and cruel. Could someone who loved melody, who loved colours, who loved not just flowers but also the leaves and stems, possibly think of a dying child as devoid of all things artistic? Did the presence of life – attached only loosely now to the tiny, withered, insignificant, uncomprehending body – possess none of the beauty of architecture? Did the spongy, unfulfilled penis oozing drops of blood have no power to spew out poetry? Was this child only a misfit riddled with disease?

There was acceptance, Ishwari's heart told her. There was, there was. Someone who went to Amsterdam in the correct season for a glimpse of tulips was bound to tell her one day, 'Yes, I should do something – before it's too late.' He would, he had to.

Mahir said, 'Now I've begun to believe, Bibaswan, that spirituality too is entertainment.'

Ishwari felt a chill as soon as she heard this. She wanted to ask, isn't art entertainment too?

'Actually, I'm confused. Sometimes I feel as though everything I've learned, everything I'm clinging to, all that gives identity to my soul is nothing but escapism.'

Bibaswan said, 'Do you mean to suggest that prehistoric cave-paintings or statues carved on the mountainside are all escapism?'

Ishwari had heard from Bibaswan that although Mahir's music was semi-classical, he had been trained from the age of seven by Ustad Ghulam Mustafa Khan of the Rampur Gharana. And his Carnatic music guru was his mother Sudhanya.

Mahir said, 'Didn't I say I'm very confused? I've been trying to find a link between art, spirituality, consciousness and everything else, Bibaswan.'

'Let me know when you do.' Bibaswan looked worried.

'I will. Look, Bib, you have to accept that I'm not the person I was ten years ago. Whatever it is I'm in search of, the quest has taken me a long way.'

'Your style has definitely changed in ten years. You're not concerned with melody at all now...'

'No, I'm not. I only think about the structure, about complicated forms. Earlier, my mood used to change during a performance but now I'm in a total state of surrender. Let the world go to hell, I think of nothing but bringing the idea of structure and form into my voice. Sometimes I don't even do that, my brain maps the entire form before I even start singing. Despite this, I am unhappy, Bibaswan.'

'Why, Mahir?'

'The most important quality for singing is intelligence. Grammar and abstraction – these two things add up to music – can anyone but an intelligent person handle these? And where are the intelligent people today in the world of music? Nowhere. Music is very insecure now. All its sentries have fallen asleep. All of them.'

'And you?'

'Who am I? I'm the lover. *Sa re ga ma pa dha ni sa*… a weak lover.'

Marize ishq ka kya hai
Jiya jiya, na jiya
Hain ek saans ka jhagda
Liya liya, na liya

Sick with love,
He doesn't care if he lives or not.
The quarrel lasts a single breath,
Who cares whether you take it or not.

Mahir sang. Bibaswan stared at him with brooding eyes.

—

They simply couldn't stop talking. Sita returned after three and forced them to have lunch. Mahir left for Nazrul Mancha at four. He requested Ishwari to tie his ponytail neatly. Before leaving, he thanked her profusely, she had no idea why.

Mahir wasn't coming back after the concert. He would spend a couple of days with a friend, also a singer, at the Sangeet Research Academy. On

Saturday, Mahir, Bibaswan and Kasturi would drive
to Santiniketan with this friend, Dhiman Karlekar.
Dhiman and Mahir were scheduled to participate
in a two-day workshop organised by the Sangeet
Research Academy. They would all stay at the house
in Gurupalli owned by Budhaditya's father. They
would return on Tuesday, and then Kasturi would fly
to Mumbai.

After Mahir left, just as Ishwari was about to ask
Bibaswan for instructions on his packing, his phone
rang. Bibaswan was lying in bed, his legs stretched out
– he was probably tired after sitting up all afternoon
with Mahir – and he answered the phone in the same
position. 'Yes, Kasturi… Yes, we had a very good
time… You know I'm crazy about him… Not coming? Why?' Then Bibaswan was silent while Kasturi
spoke continuously at the other end. Eventually he
said, 'No, it's all right, I'll go. I want to spend some
more time with Mahir.'

Kasturi wasn't going but Bibaswan was. Bibaswan
said to her, 'Will you come to Santiniketan with us,
Isha?' For a moment Ishwari was swept off her feet.
She was tempted by the thought of being with two
famous singers and Bibaswan – the most important
person in her life – the swaying of a speeding car, so
many unheard things, the music – all of it together.

The next moment she remembered how futile it was for her to try to be a part of something like this. She had a sick child at home, whom she left orphaned for much of the day in the care of a woman she only half knew. How could she leave him to go anywhere? Ishwari had no choice but to return to that room at the end of the day and to check Roo's pulse. Even Gourohori was in hospital.

She said, 'How can I go with you, Bibaswan?'

Bibaswan gave her a strange smile. 'How should I know? You're supposed to be with me. I'm not yet fit enough to move about on my own. Since Kasturi had said she would take care of me I could have done without you. But Kasturi's just cancelled, so if you don't go, I'll have to cancel too.'

'Who will I leave Roo with?'

'Oh, please, Ishwari, ask yourself this question, there's no need to embarrass me by asking. It's just that if you don't come along, I'll have to cancel this trip – that's something you must know.'

'How can you do that? You've been cooped up at home for so long. This is the first trip you've considered. You already have the company you wanted, you can't possibly not go, Bibaswan.'

'I was hoping you'd come with me, Isha. This illness, this struggle, this gradual self-depletion in body and in spirit – please come out of all this now. I want to see you once outside the walls of Radhesh-yam House. All kinds of barriers come between us here. You're always apprehensive, you look at me so wistfully, you suppress your sighs, you make me feel as though I'm the one responsible for your misery.'

Ishwari looked at Bibaswan with wide eyes, feeling excited somewhere deep within herself, wondering whether the lid was at last being taken off the most secret recesses of Bibaswan's mind. Had he realised that friendship was not a one-way affair, that even the person who paid three hundred rupees a day was capable of compassion?

She said, 'No matter what my life is like, why should you consider yourself responsible?'

At this Bibaswan pulled her close dutifully. 'I know I'm not responsible. But when I see someone suffer-ing – someone I'm so fond of – I feel like making myself suffer too. I won't ever pity you. Whatever you may think of me, none of us is worthy of being kind to others, but I will always consider your sorrows my sorrows.'

'I'll go to Santiniketan,' she declared, and they set off a day later in a Scorpio SUV. The night before that, she picked up the bedridden Roo in her arms after a long time and made him sit on the iron spiral staircase at Dinratri. They sat side by side. Roo clung hard to the railing, looking flabbergasted at the houses, the lights, the sky, the moon, the stars. She pinched her son's cheeks, kissed him, ruffled his hair. 'Do you like it here?' she asked Roo.

'Very much.'

'Do you like Kolkata?'

'A lot.'

'You don't want to go back to Mumbai? Back to them?'

'No, not at all.'

'Why not?'

Roo paused for thought. 'You know everything. It's you I like, Ma.'

'But I'm not a good mother. You're in such pain and I haven't been able to do anything about it.'

'So what?'

'Doesn't it matter?'

'I'm saying I like you because you're so bright, you shine. And when you talk… you do this thing, you do this thing… when your eyes are this way, you look even more beautiful, and when you smile… and when your hair flies this way… so pretty.' Trying to arrange her hair, Roo got it into a tangle.

'But I haven't been able to put you in a school, Roo.' Roo didn't hear her, he kept babbling, he said she smelled good, he said he felt sleepy as soon as Ishwari lay down next to him…

Eventually she told her son she wouldn't be home for two days. She would be working very hard for those two days. She smothered him in kisses, saying, 'Will you be a good boy? You won't be naughty?'

Roo said, 'I'm always lying down like a good boy, Ma, am I ever naughty? Ask Preeti.'

Then Roo began to sing 'All the Lonely People', swaying in time with the tune.

Ah, look at all those lonely people
Where do they all belong?

'You remember?' she said in surprise.

'What did you think?' Roo smiled. He asked, 'Do you know what I think of when I hear this song, Ma?'

She said, 'Tell me, what do you think? Whatever you say before being wiped away, that's literature, darling!'

Roo said, 'I think of something like a village… No one lives there any more, all the houses are empty. There's a church, its bell is broken. And there's a stable, no horses in it but just skeletons of horses, with strange plants entwined in their bones.' Ishwari sat in silence until Roo spoke again. 'I want to listen to music, Ma.'

'Music? Do you want The Beatles?'

'No, Ma, some music that lasts longer.'

'What kind of music?'

'Music that will continue playing even after I'm gone, it won't end...'

'I don't know any music that plays so long, Roo. But you can listen to Tchaikovsky's "Dance of the Swans".'

'Will I be cured if I do, Ma?'

'No, but like you said,' her lips trembled, 'it will keep playing even when you're gone.'

'Sing it then.'

'How do I sing it, Roo? This isn't Indian classical music. It is Western classical, there's very little voice in it, it isn't for singing, it's for feeling. I can only describe it for you.'

'Then do that, Ma.'

And so Ishwari described the dance of the swans. 'Just imagine, Roo, suddenly the moonlight falls like rain, you and I are sitting here, the terrace is flooded by light, it spreads — it comes all the way up to these stairs, dazzling, and at that moment four milk-white swans descend from the skies. They begin to dance in circles... they dance, they stop and wave their wings, dripping moonlight, then dance again, dance in circles, then stop… They dedicate to you what they have, what you and I don't. They dance until you fall asleep, until you float away like a feather as far as you have to go.'

—

It was ten by the time they drove into Santiniketan. The car took a right turn at Bhubandanga. Pointing to the left, Bibaswan said, 'All this is part of the ashram. The summer vacation probably hasn't begun. Take a walk by yourself in the evening and look around. My grandfather had forced me to go to the Ananda school for about six months. I still remember those days. One of the teachers walked about barefoot, and she would tuck into her hair anything her students gave her. Someone might give her a clump of grass or a dry twig or even a feather, and she would accept it with a smile and tuck it into her hair. I remember her clearly. It would have been better if I had come here after my mother died instead of going to Gwalior. I have no doubt I would have emerged as a painter in that case.'

'But you have emerged,' said Mahir. 'Your portrait of Ishwari is incredible.'

'I'm an untrained artist. In fact, I can't even call myself an artist. In my case painting is just emotional

escapism. As long as I paint I settle scores with myself;
as soon as the painting's finished, so is my relationship with it. There's something else that happens
– say I'm painting a portrait of my mother, forgotten
moments we spent together come back to me, it's the
same when painting Tania. I remembered the other
day that Tania used a blue sling bag with mirrorwork
when she was at Sophia College. It was a beautiful
bag. I've decided to paint Tania, that sling bag, and a
dead puppy inside the bag.'

The car stopped in front of a house painted a sooth-
ing shade of pastel brown. It was a very old house, but
extremely well-maintained, and Sita's touch was evident everywhere. One entire wall was covered in ivy
vines. The house was set in a huge compound with
all kinds of trees. Whoever had planned this garden
had meant it to be a little haphazard and disorgan-
ised, so that it appeared romantic and mysterious.
Mahir was on the phone, his troop hadn't arrived
in Bolpur yet. Sukhendu and the caretaker had carried Bibaswan upstairs. Mahir and Dhiman Karlekar
would leave for the workshop as soon as they had
bathed. Visva-Bharati would arrange for their lunch.
Sukhendu would cook an afternoon meal for Ishwari and Bibaswan. Ishwari had been given the room
next to Bibaswan's. The windows in her room looked

onto beckoning ivy vines on one side, and on the other side she could glimpse a tall barbed wire fence through gaps in the trees, beyond it the compound of another house.

As soon as Ishwari was alone she thought of Roo and unhappiness pricked at her heart like a swarm of ants. She had covered a great distance with this journey. The terrace of Dinratri was just four hours away, but already it felt indistinct. Roo was the greatest obstacle in Ishwari's torn existence but she had never imagined, while roving between Dinratri and Radheshyam and the hospital and doctors and reports and pharmacies, that she could spend a day without Roo. Ishwari had requested Rantideb and Bibaswan to open a bank account for her. They had been unable to help, so she constantly carried the money she had saved for Roo's treatment, and had brought it with her here – while Roo was left alone. Perhaps Preeti was scolding him for refusing to eat his starchy rice. For a moment she wondered whether she really did want to weep because she had left Roo behind. Was a process of love indeed at work within her constantly, trying to safeguard Roo? Or had the apathy borne out of bearing Roo's burden actually strengthened at the taste of travel?

She wondered why Roo was alive despite such

neglect. Such prolonged starvation, so much powerful medication – how did his eyes shine so bright last
night?

Ishwari had left her phone with Preeti. Before
bathing, she went to Bibaswan's room to borrow his
to talk to Roo, and the moment she appeared Bibaswan put his arms around her and drew her to him.
She didn't even get a chance to protest.

—

The house grew indifferent and cold as the afternoon
wore on. Lying on Bibaswan's black and green bedspread, Ishwari observed her naked reflection in the
mirror, the nude man sitting cross-legged at her feet
ignoring the pain in his legs – the preamble to the
instant before entering her. He filled her vagina with
his finger, and at that moment she wished the mirror
would turn opaque.

Bibaswan explored her physically before plunging
into the foam, and suddenly Ishwari found herself able
to touch silence in its totality. She tried to freeze into
pain while feeling the pressure of a broken, dead lever
within herself. She felt an upheaval in her head – she
thought she would forget all her stories this instant.

At one point Bibaswan told her, 'Concentrate,
Ishwari, concentrate. Give me your attention.'

She wanted to say something, but the hoofbeats dragged time on. Bibaswan tried to arouse her somnolent breasts, and told her, 'We won't get this time back.'

'I know,' she whispered, 'art and death do not go together.'

A pain far greater than the one Bibaswan had tried to inflict on Ishwari dribbled within her, and she felt the agony of struggling uphill, uphill and even further uphill.

Bibaswan smothered her in kisses, saying, 'You're just like Mallikarjun Mansoor singing "Bilaskhani Todi", Isha.' His words set her belly and thighs ablaze. Half an hour later Bibaswan and she lay side by side. Spurred by a thought, Bibaswan put his clothes on. Ishwari remained undressed – she saw nothing unusual in this outcome, she only recollected the irksome, wary conversation between her and Bibaswan on the first day. Circling her nipples with his finger, Bibaswan had said, 'You're so repressed, Ishwari.'

'Why?'

'You talk such rubbish all day, but you don't make a sound during sex.'

'What does that prove?'

'It proves that you've hidden things deep inside you, secret truths, and no matter how clever a sto-

ryteller you may be, you're actually a complete
introvert. A woman of your age should be screaming
loud enough for people to gather around.'

'So this is what you make of life, Bibaswan?' she
said. 'A room next to another, and yet another, a room
full of people, a house of people – does life only mean
the sea-facing flat you and Tania lived in? Here most
people, men and women, have sex with their hands
clamped over one another's mouths, tiptoeing to the
bathroom afterwards. Sexuality is still a matter of faith
to people in this country, it's not something you do.'

Bibaswan was taken aback. 'Perhaps you're right.
We're so detached that we know nothing about such
lives. The very thought of a married couple having sex while their baby lies next to them makes my
stomach turn. I wouldn't even manage an erection
in such a situation. Sex means complete freedom – if
there's a baby in the room... I don't know! Have you
ever had sex with your son in the room?'

Ishwari sat up to go to the toilet, she returned
to find Bibaswan somewhat distracted. His eyes were
glazed as he turned to her. 'Why is Dalí your lover,
Ishwari?' he asked.

Ishwari looked at the skylight that revealed the
last sunlight of the day, enough to fill the silent, air-
conditioned room.

'Dalí? "I don't know when I start pretending or when I speak the truth." This confession of Dali attracted me to him the first time I heard it – someone who didn't know when he was acting and when he was telling the truth – that is the true artist. Dalí – the Cosmic Rhinoceros. I was convinced by the vibrating pile of bricks that time would be born again, a new time. I'm still crazy about his intelligent soul. I don't believe there is a Dalí in this world any more, Bibaswan – someone who can paint a 'Premonition of Civil War' or an 'Autumn Cannibalism' whenever he wants to. How fantastic Dalí's mind was, it is bound to be one of the wonders of the world. An evening with Gala on the coast of Spain, their first kiss – who wouldn't be astounded to know that an incident such as this was behind the creation of 'Autumn Cannibalism', Bibaswan? I know my trite life will reach a surreal culmination one day, and surely Dalí will come to my help then.'

—

Mahir and Dhiman Karlekar returned in the late afternoon. Everyone gathered in Bibaswan's room for tea. Bibaswan had been present here once as Ali Akbar Khan's satellite. With narrowed eyes he described the almost supernatural experience he had had during

Khan Sahib's three-day workshop and threw annoyed glances at Ishwari from time to time. The reason for the annoyance: despite reminders, she had forgotten to bring her white Dhakai sari. She was hovering around Bibaswan this Santiniketan evening in a black kurta. Ishwari laughed, for in the folds of irritation in Bibaswan's eyes she could see the sting of desire.

A little later a group of professors from Sangeet Bhavan escorted Mahir and Dhiman to another gathering.

Ishwari undressed as soon as they left. Once again Bibaswan kept telling her to concentrate. 'Where has your mind drifted, Ishwari? Tell me what I mean to you. Kiss me. I cannot make out whether you want me at all. Show me, talk to me.' Bibaswan forced her lips apart and sucked on her tongue. Still she couldn't start a conversation. Finally Bibaswan exclaimed, 'You're so secretive! Calculating, shrewd – I know you.'

'Why?' Ishwari spoke at last.

'You're here, you're having sex with me, and you can't tell me even once what you like about me. You cannot say even once, "I love you".'

She lapsed into silence again.

'I haven't had sex for at least a year and a half – do you know that?' Bibaswan said.

'You are completely cured, Bibaswan,' she told

him. 'Your life lies ahead of you now, a new, unfet-
tered life.'

'And you?'

'I have to look for another job.'

'It's no lie that I love you, Isha,' Bibaswan said. 'I
don't want to leave you, you're all I need, all my ego
needs. But I cannot accept your child.'

'No one is willing to accept another's child as his
own,' she responded.

'What do you mean?'

'Have you ever read the matrimonial columns,
Bibaswan? Everyone beckons to the "unencumbered". The widower, the divorced, even the father
of two – one aged seven, the other ten – are looking for the unencumbered, no one's willing to take
responsibility for anyone else. Society will not throw
up one person who will stand by you when you're
in trouble, it will not provide a single person willing to introduce you to others. Society is filled with
nothing but people who are afraid – and yet how the
ranks of the artists swell by the day! Every single day
seventy new singers are born, forty people have painting exhibitions and thousands of people – those very
people who wish to remain unencumbered – identify
with this art. On lazy afternoons at the club, everyone's using explicit art, monotheism, consciousness

and surrealism as chasers for their beer and pakodas.'

—

Mahir and Dhiman were absent on Sunday evening too.

Bibaswan said, 'I like you, just you and you. And here it ends.' She listened in silence, picking at Bibaswan's dried semen on her belly like dried dandruff. Bibaswan's voice became progressively calmer. 'I can't be a father to your child, Ishwari. My family will not accept him.'

Ten minutes later he said, 'You're right from your standpoint. You need someone who's willing to accept you with your child. I'm sure you'll find someone like that.'

Twenty minutes later, 'Do you know what a family means, Ishwari?'

An hour later, 'Your childhood, your son's childhood – what is he passing through? I am afraid. Already I feel scared to be here with you.'

Three hours later, 'You hate art. You… you hate me too. You have no compassion for me.'

A day later, 'Do you think that just because your son's dying without treatment, you're the only one to have a claim on art? Shut up!'

A day and seven hours later, 'Dalí? You love Dalí?

That genius of ugliness? How can you stand that painting? 'Child Eating a Rat'? Who's been given ten out of ten for perversity? Love for nature but none for children? Did you know that? Form? Yes. Go, woman, go. Now please leave me alone.'

—

The day she returned, Gourohori died. The very same hour. 'Take care of Roo,' he told her. 'Don't let go of him.' Roo had to be hospitalised the next day. He needed a blood transfusion, saline too. For eight days he had stared death in the face. And on one of those days Preeti told her with a bowed head that she was leaving. Sukul and she were going to get married and settle down in Orissa. Sukul had been offered a well-paid job there.

Preeti left without even meeting Roo. She had realised the futility of letting the attachment grow. On the twelfth day, locking Roo in the room again, Ishwari appeared at Radheshyam House. Sita was delighted to see her. 'Bibaswan's in Bangalore, didn't he tell you? There's so much still to be done in his new flat. I'm going tomorrow. I'm trying to find a good job for you here, Ishwari. Even Bibaswan has asked me to be on the lookout. Keep this envelope. I've made provisions for today too. You can keep the phone too, just return the SIM card to me, since it's registered in Bibaswan's name. And call me if you ever need anything, all right? You're trying for a job too, aren't you?'

Gourohori's room was occupied by a newcomer from Nikhil Biswas's hometown; he was the new doorman at Dinratri.

Rantideb had gone abroad, according to Nikhil. One evening, she set off after dusk with Roo. They took a taxi to the river. After paying the driver, she walked along the bridge, Roo on her shoulder. And then she sat down on the ground, dangling her legs over the water through the broken railing. She made Roo sit too. The water sparkled in pools where the light fell on it. After some time she confessed, 'I can't cope with you any more, Roo.'

Roo nodded as though he understood, then said, 'I won't be naughty any more, Ma. I'll be cured completely. I won't vomit. I won't say my stomach or hips are aching. If I vomit I'll clean it up myself. I won't get a fever, I promise, Ma. Can't you give me all the medicine in one go?'

'Do you know what dying means?' she asked him. Roo shook his head. He shook it impatiently, as though, if he had to be told, he wanted to be told right now. Ishwari looked at the water, her well-wisher, flowing forty feet beneath them.

'Let's go, Ma,' Roo said. 'I can't keep sitting any longer.'

'Go where?'

'Wherever you're going, Ma, nowhere else.' Roo was afraid.

He had to be hospitalised again that night. Her entire savings were being eroded in a few days. Rantideb telephoned to say that Bibaswan was buying Dinratri from him. It would re-emerge as an advanced academy for semi-classical music under the combined initiative of Mahir and Bibaswan. Therefore Rantideb no longer had any time to spare for Ishwari. She disconnected the phone after thanking him for all that he had done for her. An aggressive change was at once evident in Nikhil Biswas's behaviour. With all opposition gone, he began drinking on the terrace stairs every evening, surrounded by his friends.

When Roo was discharged from the hospital she noticed that, despite all his handicaps, Roo had grown a little. Just a little, but even that was a lot for a mother like her.

—

Ishwari dressed Roo in his best clothes one afternoon. 'Where are we going today, Ma?' he asked.

'To a village fair,' she replied.

Ishwari and Roo had never been to a village fair together. They boarded an almost empty train, there were barely three or four people in the compartment. Roo fell asleep in her lap as soon as they sat down. The train tore through the terrain towards the other half of the world, in keeping with the assumptions and tendencies of this novel. Like art racing towards excellence, it raced across the earth. When the train slowed down to a crawl, and came to a virtual stand-still, Ishwari spotted a fair in full swing – just the kind she was looking for. Clutching Roo to her breast, she jumped off the train and ran across the railway lines and across the field. She made her way through the tall grass and arrived amid a crowd of unfamiliar fairground visitors from the hinterland. Hundreds of voices, clamour, buying and selling among jalebis and sweets, Ferris wheels and merry-go-rounds. Rubbing his eyes, Roo jumped out of her arms. He tried to approach something that had caught his attention, pulling her along. The crowds collided with them noisily, jostling them in different directions, none of them familiar to her. 'Ma,' Roo called out.

They walked towards a little girl who was danc-ing, and stopped to watch her. Darkness descended slowly; the sky turned red on one side, purple on the other. The musician accompanying the little dancing girl beat his drum loudly. The sounds rose towards the sky and fell back to the earth under their own weight.

Ishwari did nothing. She only loosened her grip – there in that fair she loosened her meaningless grip on relationships, on responsibility, on love, on trust, on duties, loosened her hold on her right to life. Roo went further ahead and she retreated. And being a virtual human being, she felt no pain, for she knew that every artist had to sacrifice her soul at one time or another in order to keep living as a practised, professional entertainer.

ACKNOWLEDGEMENTS

The publisher would like to acknowledge the use of the following materials:

Page 8: Friedrich Nietzsche, *Die fröhliche Wissenschaft* (The Gay Science, 1882)

Pages 67–69: T.S. Eliot, 'Rhapsody on a Windy Night', *Prufrock and Other Observations* (1920)

Page 114: Khalil Gibran, *The Prophet* (1923)

Page 176: Nadine Gordimer, *My Son's Story* (Bloomsbury Publishing Plc., 1990) reproduced with permission from the publisher.

Page 170: Keki Daruwalla, 'Going Down the Night River', *Night River and Other Poems* (Rupa and Co., 2001) reproduced with permission from the poet.

The origins of the ghazals reproduced on pages 141, 142, 146, 156, 159, 160, 162, 163 and 205 could not be traced.

This edition published in the United Kingdom by Tilted Axis Press in 2017, by arrangement with HarperCollins India.

tiltedaxispress.com

First published in Bengali by Ananda Publishers Pvt Ltd in 2013.

ISBN (paperback)   9781911284116
ISBN (ebook)   9781911284109

A catalogue record for this book is available from the British Library.

Edited by Saba Ahmed
Cover design by Soraya Gilanni Viljoen
Typesetting and ebook production by Simon Collinson
Printed and bound by CPI Group (UK) Ltd, Croydon, CR0 4YY

Supported using public funding by
**ARTS COUNCIL
ENGLAND**

ABOUT TILTED AXIS PRESS

Founded in 2015 and based in Sheffield and London, Tilted Axis is a not-for-profit press on a mission to shake up contemporary international literature.

Tilted Axis publishes the books that might not otherwise make it into English, for the very reasons that make them exciting to us – artistic originality, radical vision, the sense that here is something new.

Tilting the axis of world literature from the centre to the margins allows us to challenge that very division. These margins are spaces of compelling innovation, where multiple traditions spark new forms and translation plays a crucial role.

As part of carving out a new direction in the publishing industry, Tilted Axis is also dedicated to improving access. We're proud to pay our translators the proper rate, and to operate without unpaid interns.

We hope you find this fantastic book as thrilling and beguiling as we do, and if you do, we'd love to know.

tiltedaxispress.com
@TiltedAxisPress